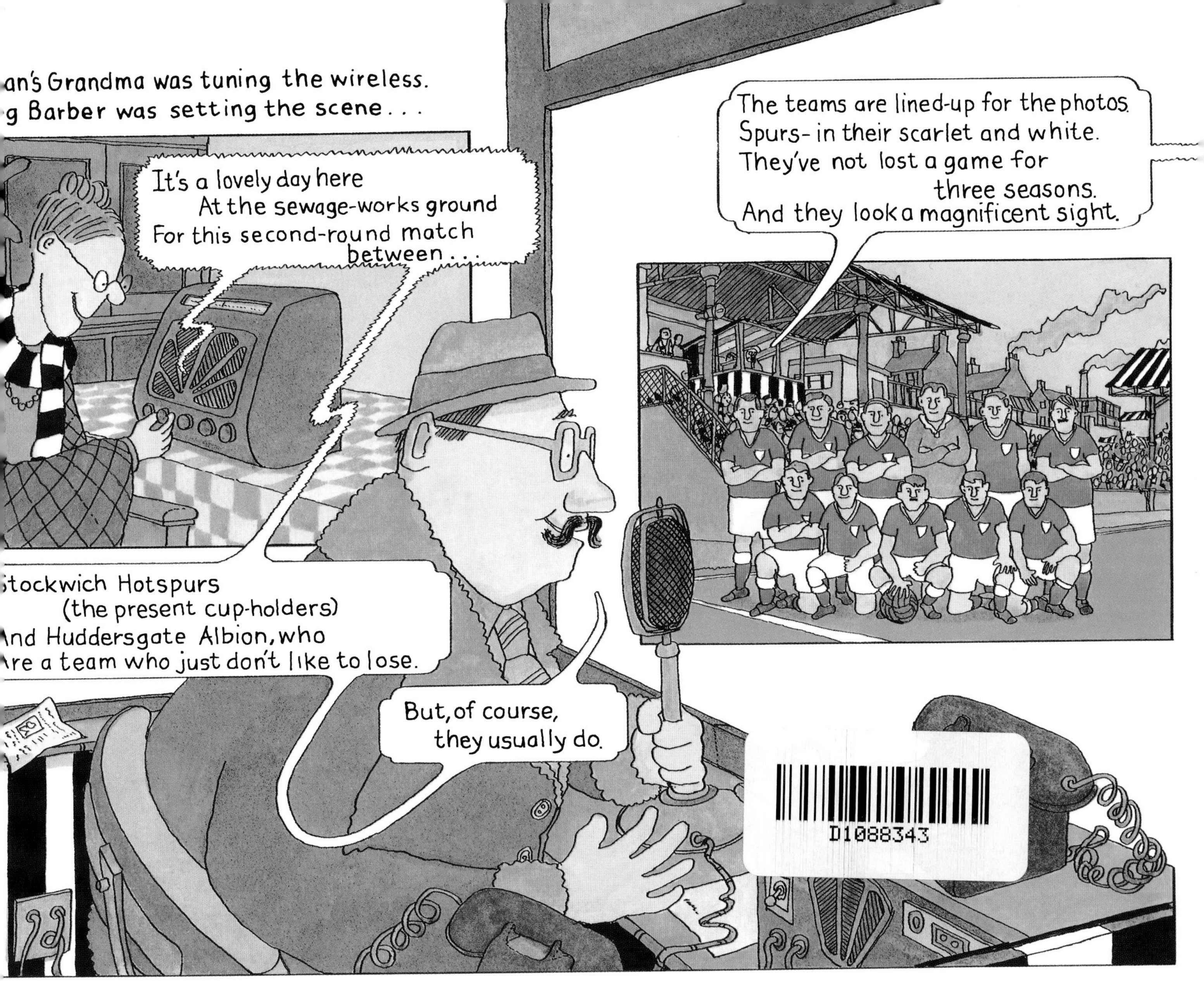
an's Grandma was tuning the wireless.
g Barber was setting the scene . . .
It's a lovely day here At the sewage-works ground For this second-round match between . . .
tockwich Hotspurs (the present cup-holders) nd Huddersgate Albion, who re a team who just don't like to lose.
But, of course, they usually do.
The teams are lined-up for the photos. Spurs- in their scarlet and white. They've not lost a game for three seasons. And they look a magnificent sight.

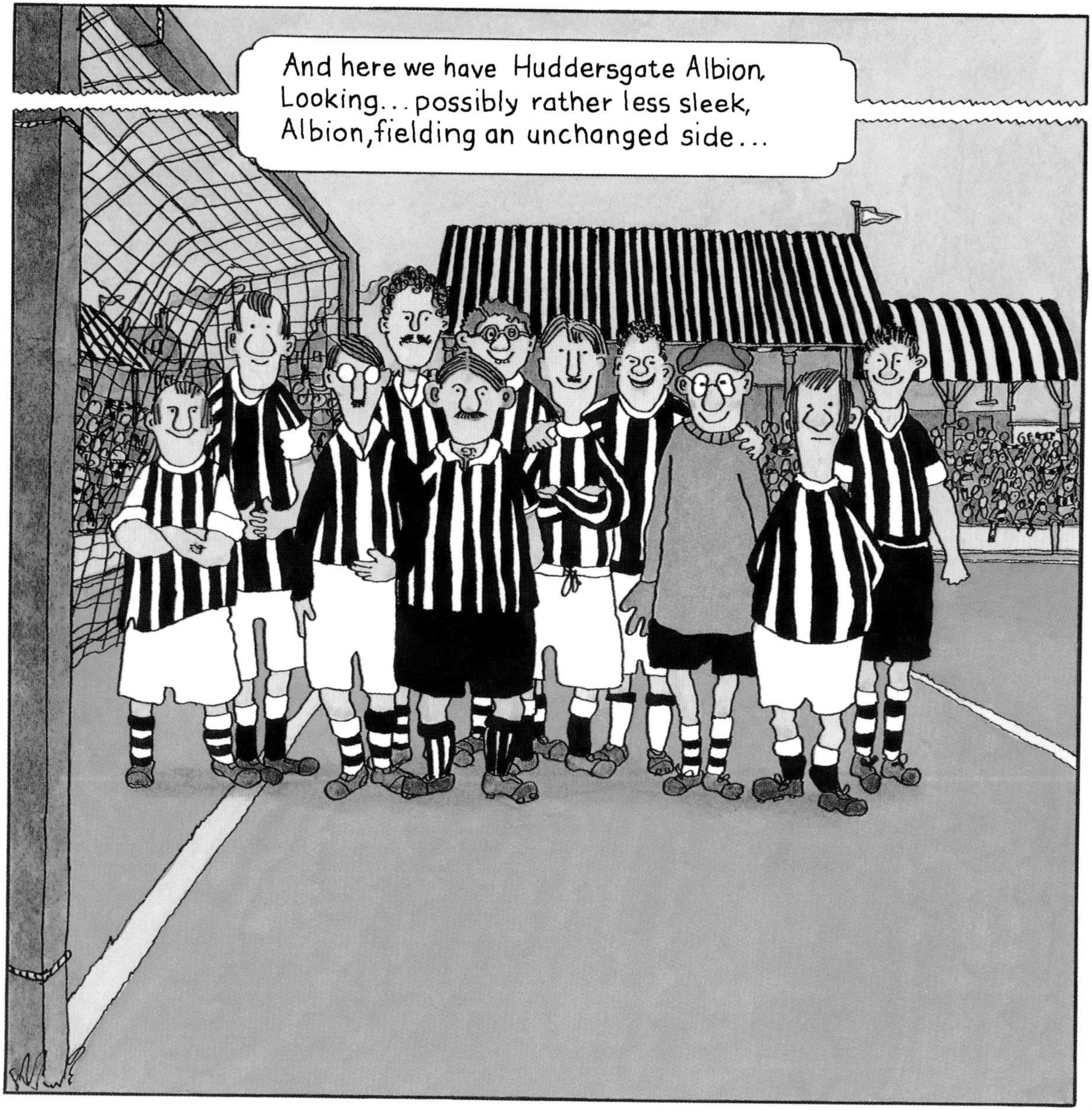
And here we have Huddersgate Albion, Looking... possibly rather less sleek, Albion, fielding an unchanged side...

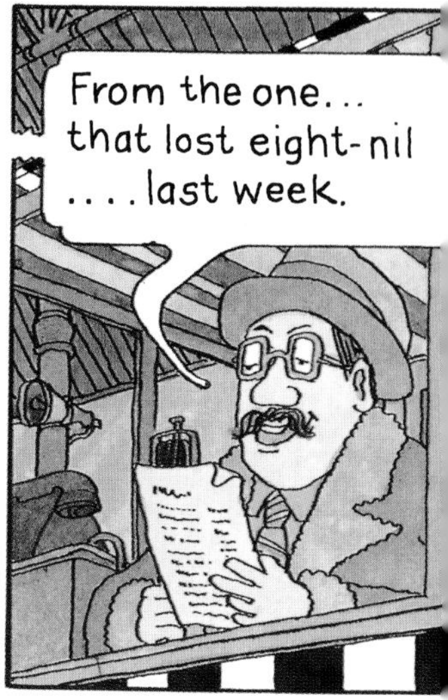
From the one... that lost eight-nil ....last week.

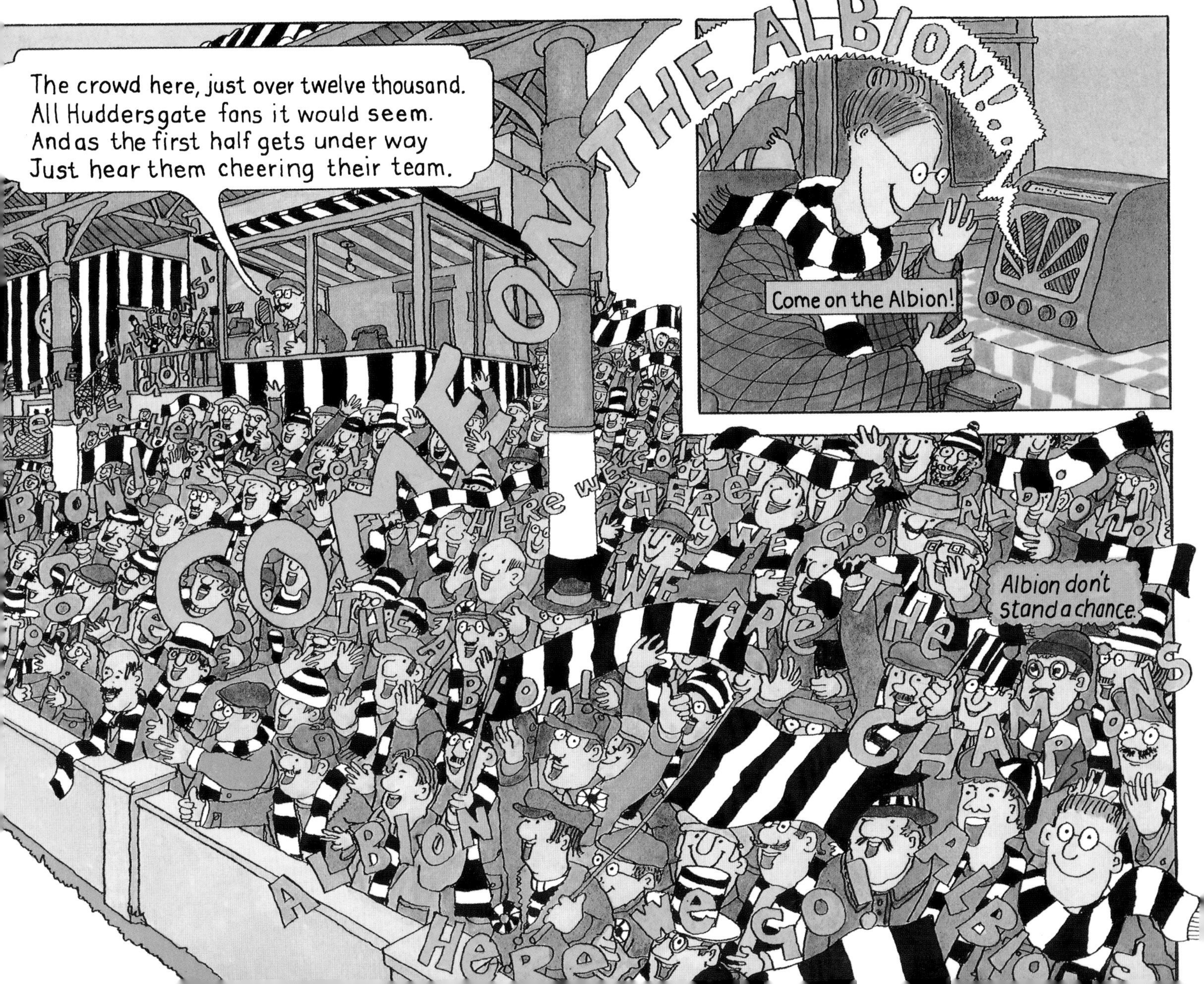
The crowd here, just over twelve thousand.
All Huddersgate fans it would seem.
And as the first half gets under way
Just hear them cheering their team.
COME ON THE ALBION!!
Come on the Albion!
HERE WE GO!
WE ARE THE CHAMPIONS
Albion don't stand a chance.

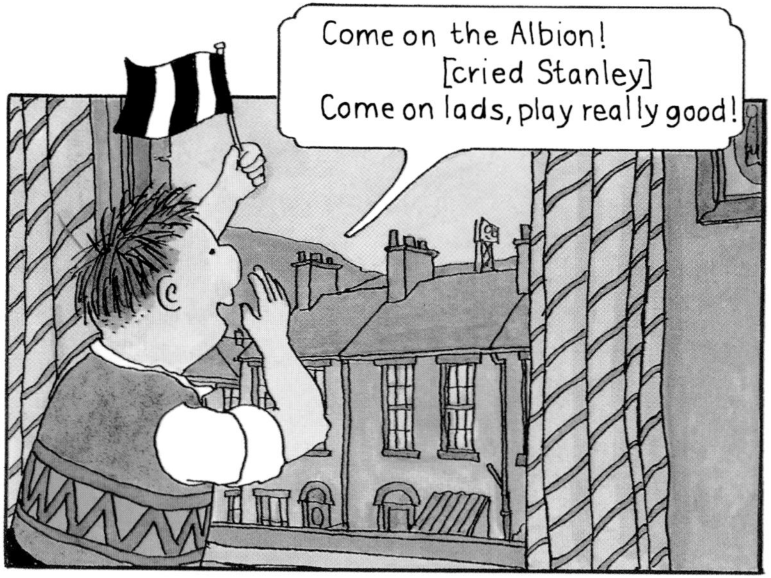
Come on the Albion!
[cried Stanley]
Come on lads, play really good!

The sewage-works ground was quite far away,
So he shouted as loud as he could.

But after a while it seemed pointless.
The team couldn't hear him, and so . . .

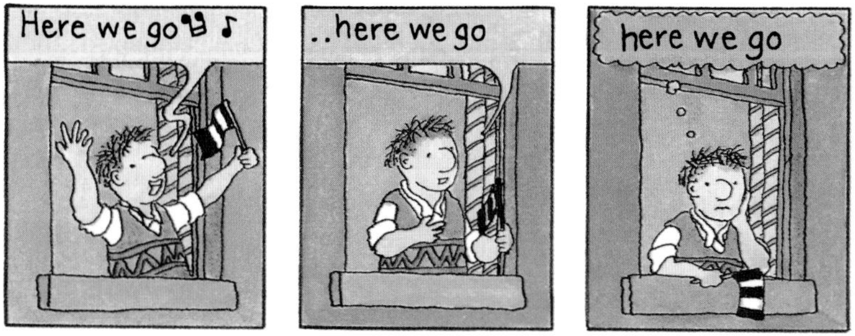
Here we go
..here we go
here we go

He just gazed out the back bedroom window,

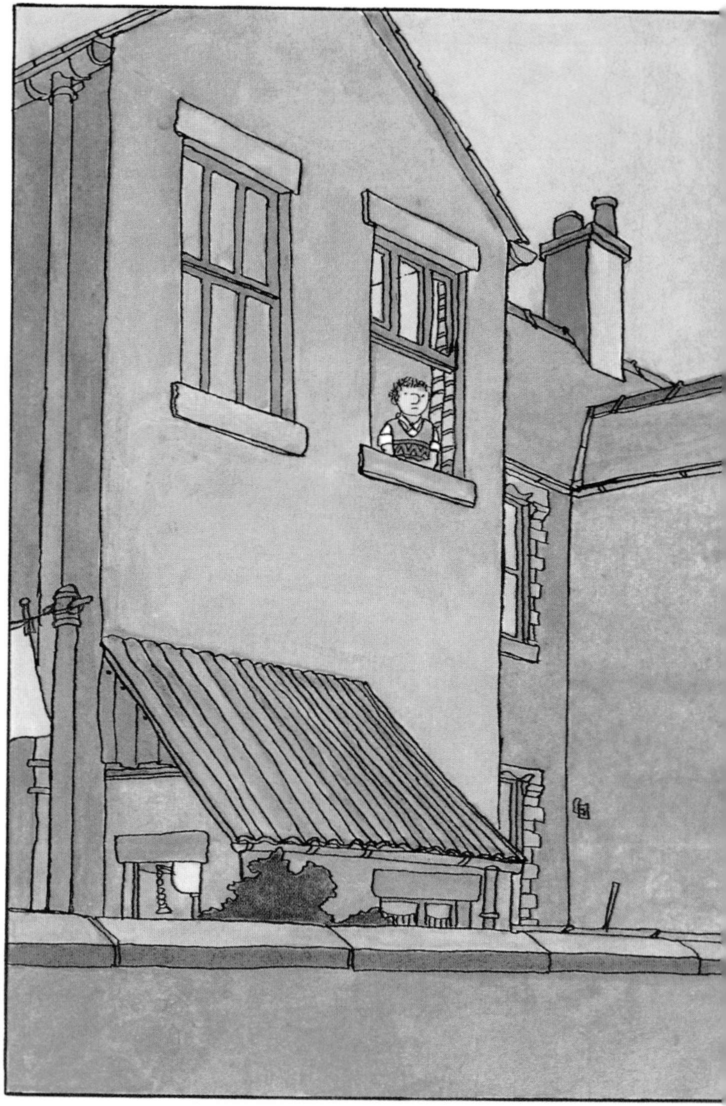

And the time... seemed to pass... very slow

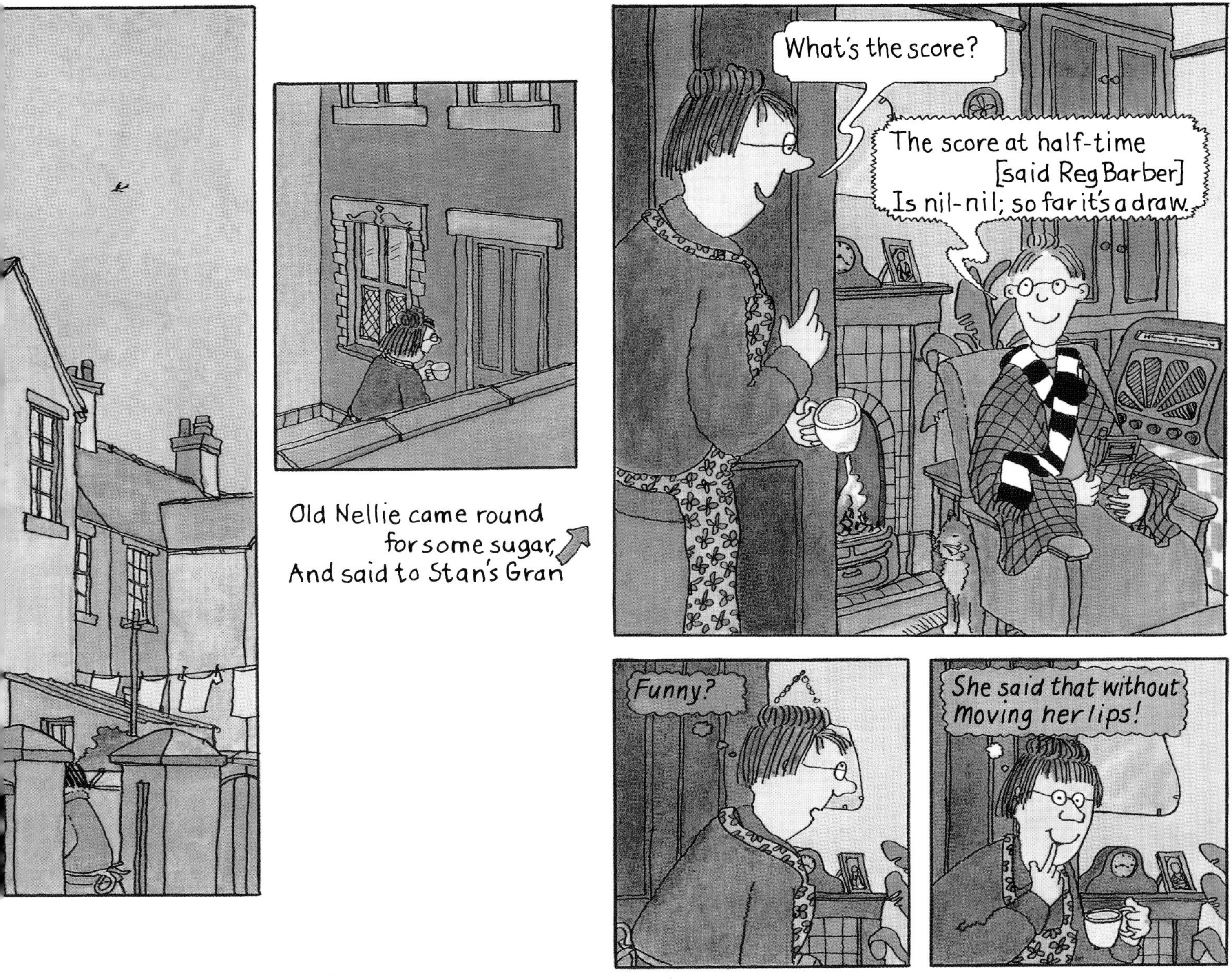
Old Nellie came round
for some sugar,
And said to Stan's Gran
What's the score?
The score at half-time
[said Reg Barber]
Is nil-nil; so far it's a draw.
Funny?
She said that without moving her lips!

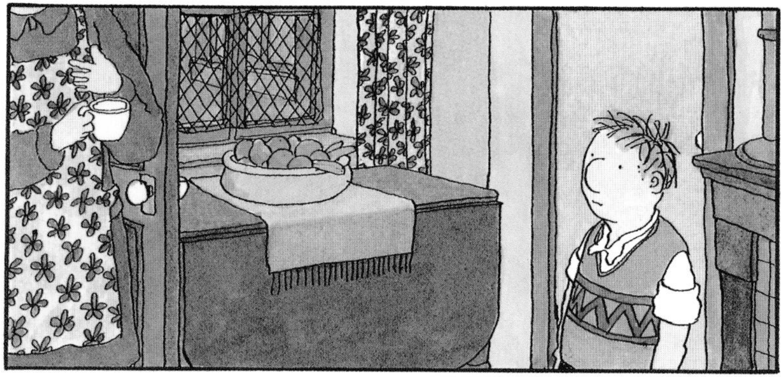

Our Stanley appeared in the doorway,

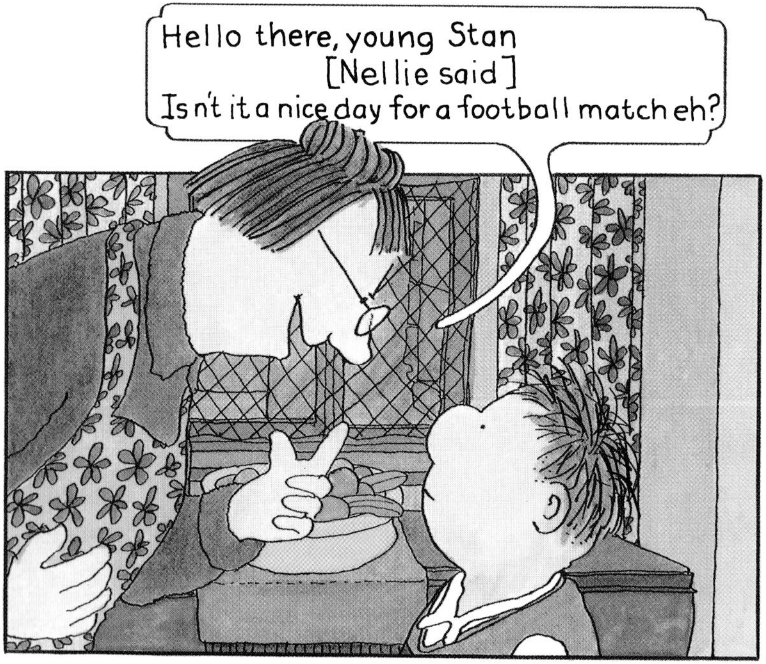
Hello there, young Stan [Nellie said] Isn't it a nice day for a football match eh?

Our Stanley just nodded his head.

But Grandma knew how Stan was feeling
And said to him . . .

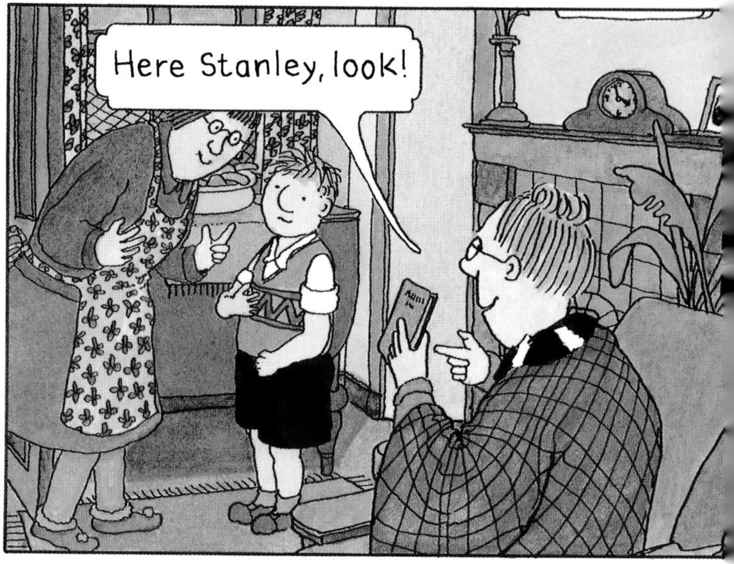
Here Stanley, look!

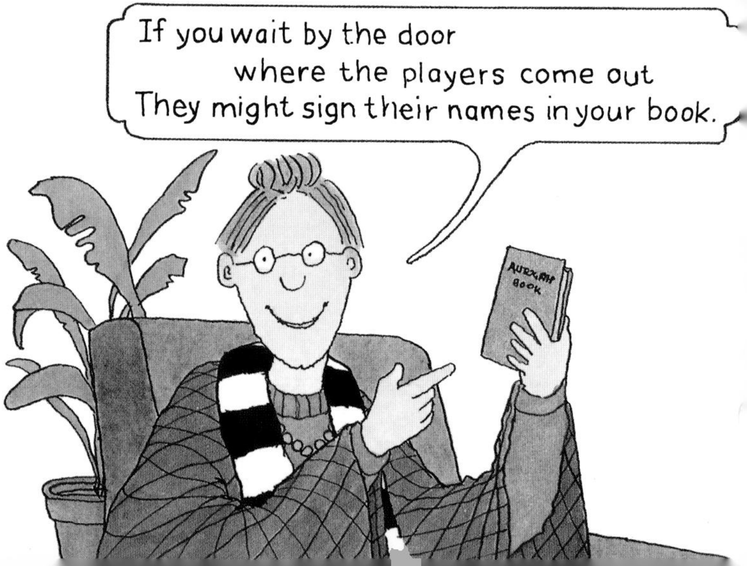
If you wait by the door where the players come out They might sign their names in your book.

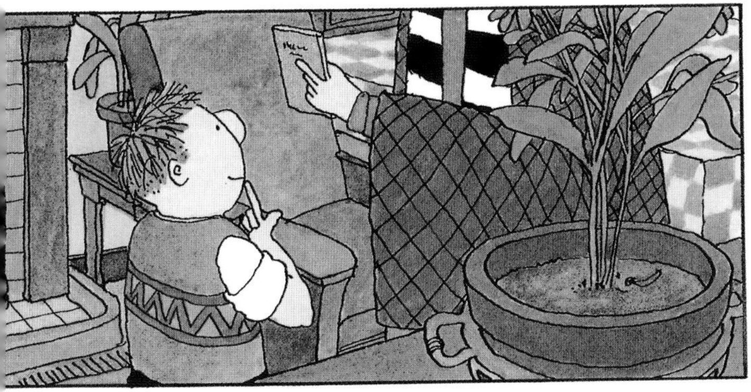

Now, Stanley collected autographs,
But so far he'd only got three:-
His Auntie Ann; the insurance man,
And a lady he'd met in Torquay.

But the 'Spurs' players were *really* famous.
Wayne Flacket - he was world-renowned.

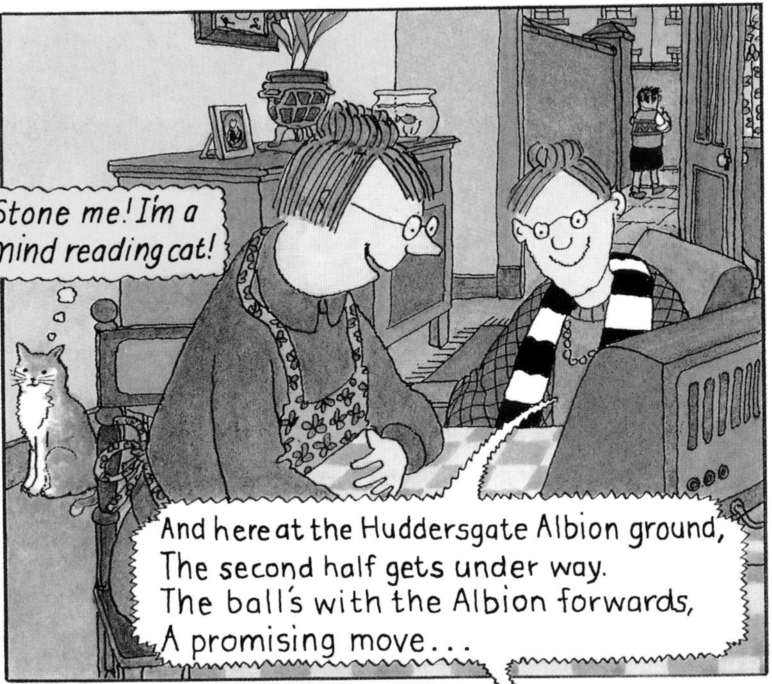
Stone me! I'm a mind reading cat!
And here at the Huddersgate Albion ground, The second half gets under way. The ball's with the Albion forwards, A promising move...

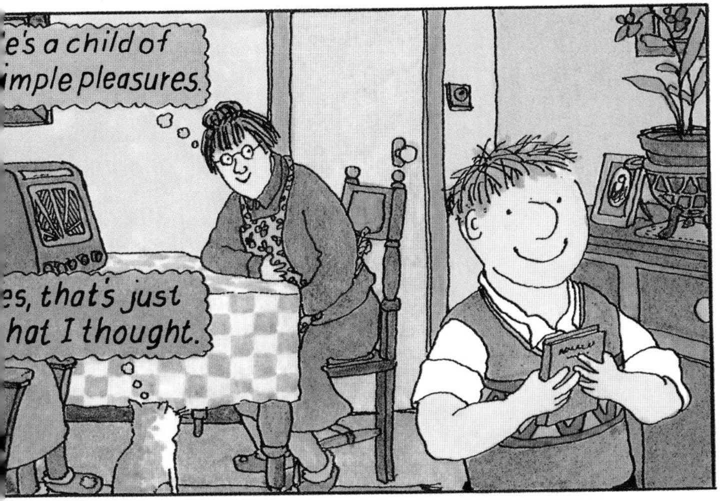
e's a child of imple pleasures.
es, that's just hat I thought.

So, clutching his autograph book in his hand,
Our Stanley set off for the ground.

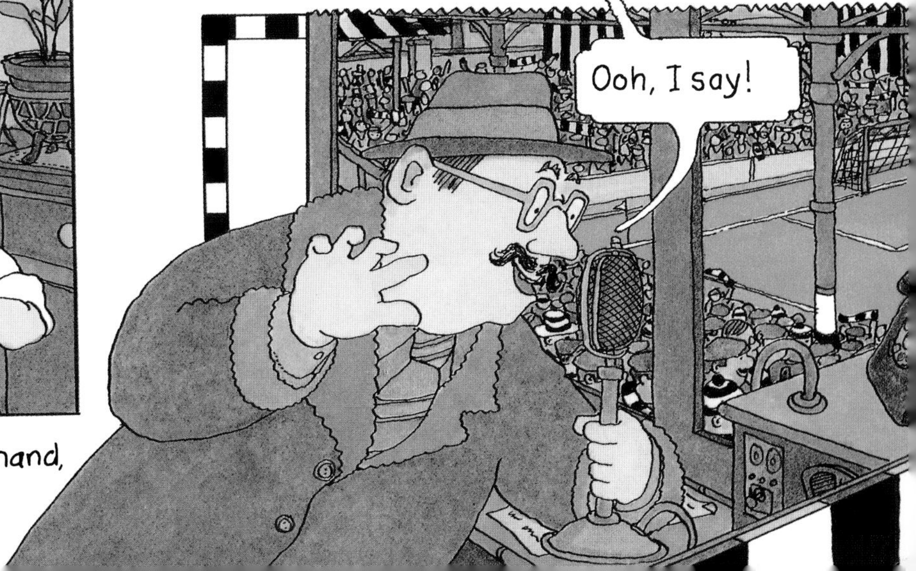
Ooh, I say!

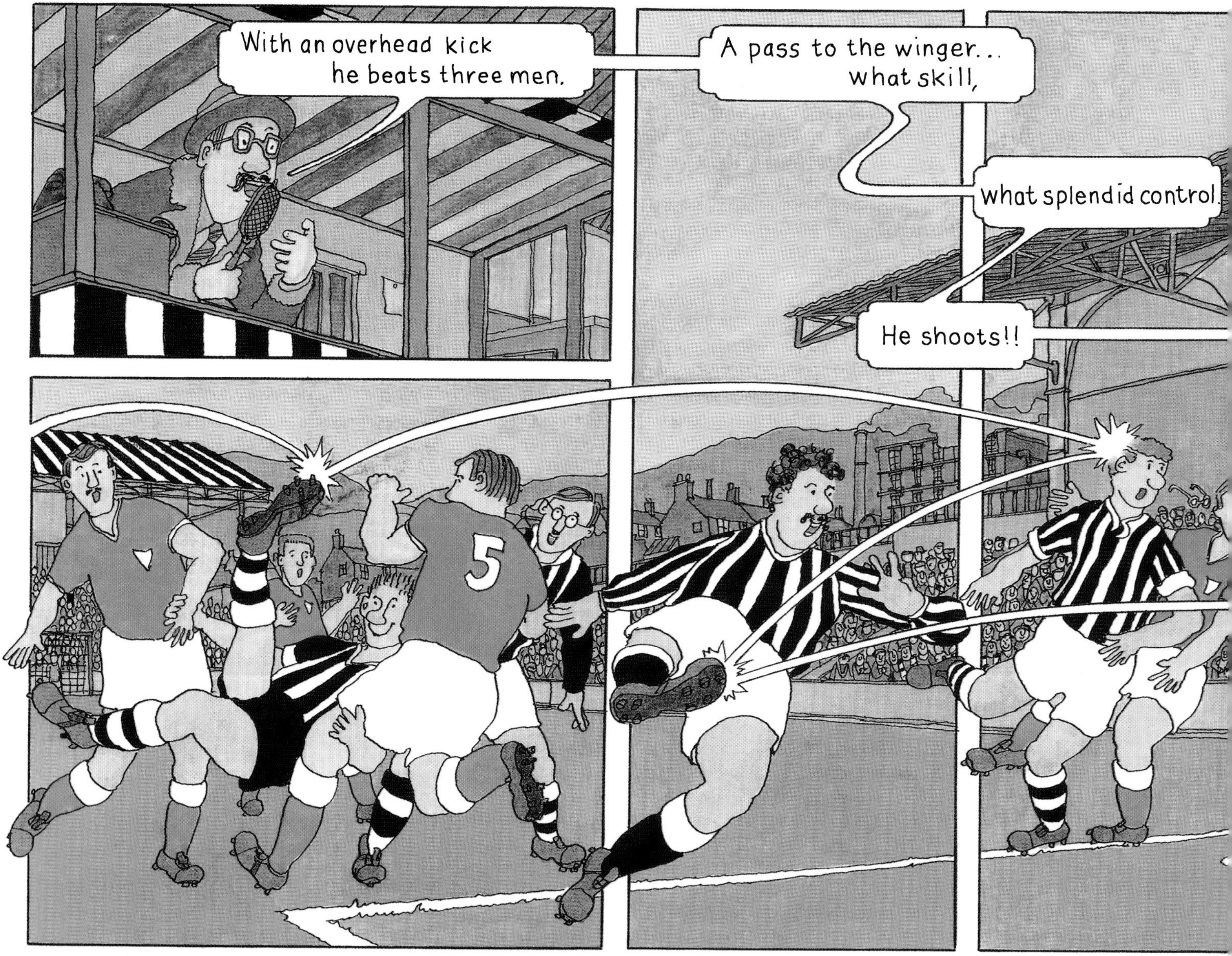

With an overhead kick he beats three men.
A pass to the winger... what skill,
what splendid control.
He shoots!!
5

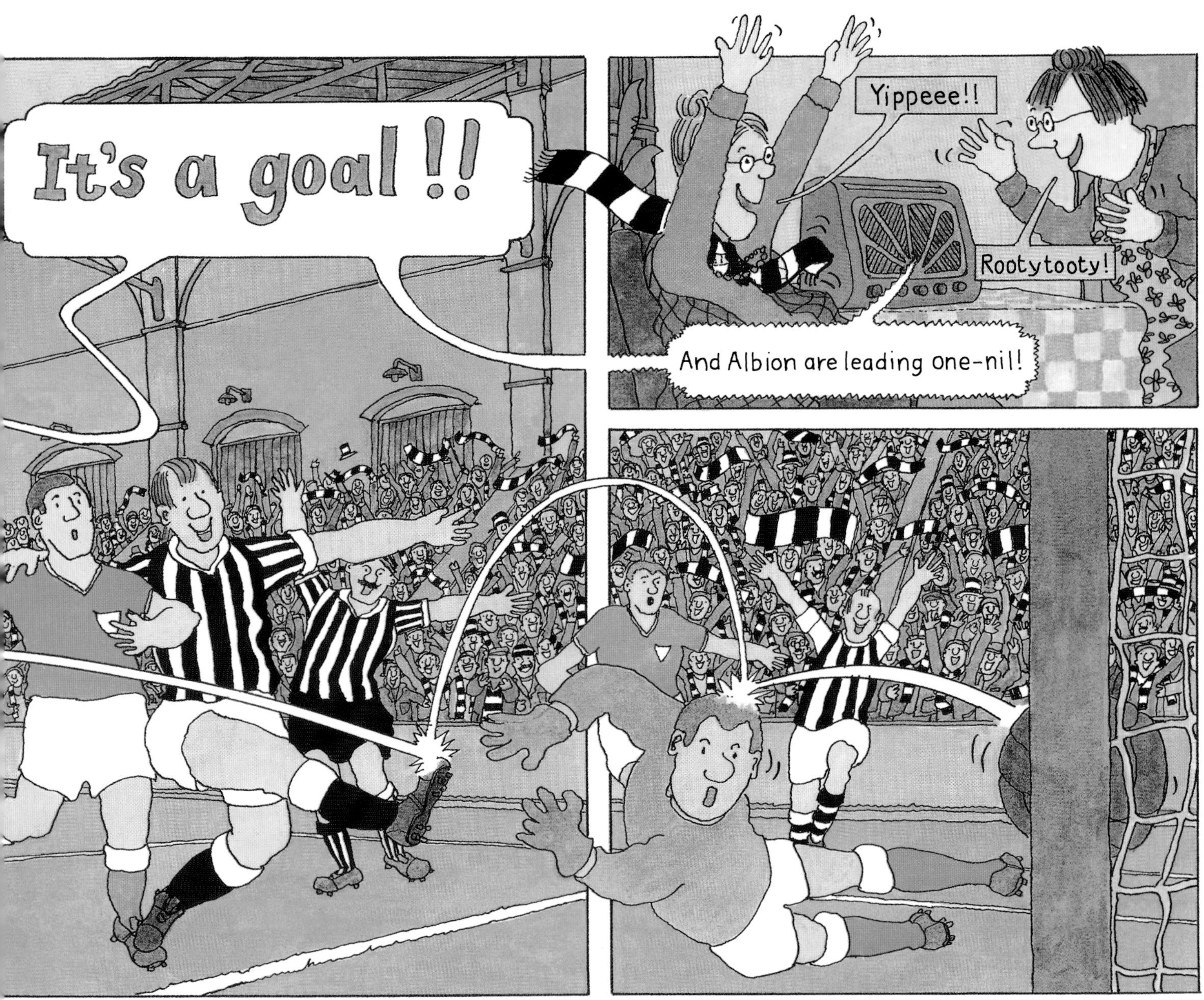
It's a goal !!
Yippeee!!
Rootytooty!
And Albion are leading one-nil!

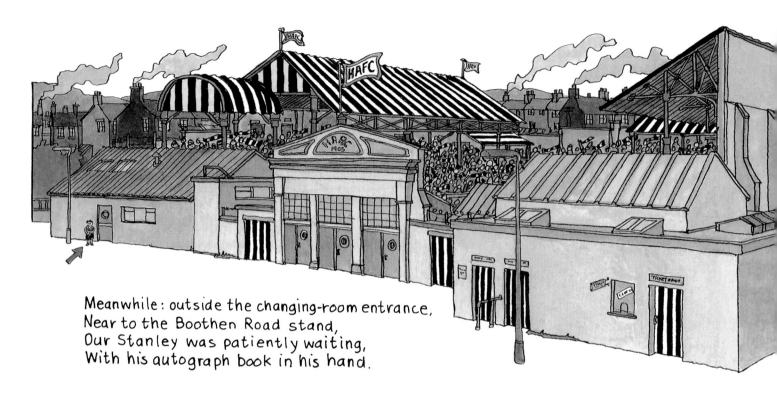

Meanwhile: outside the changing-room entrance,
Near to the Boothen Road stand,
Our Stanley was patiently waiting,
With his autograph book in his hand.

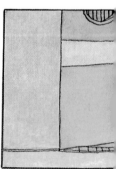

Now, the changing room door was open a bit,
And this was temptation to Stan.

He just couldn't keep from taking a
And that's how the real fun beg

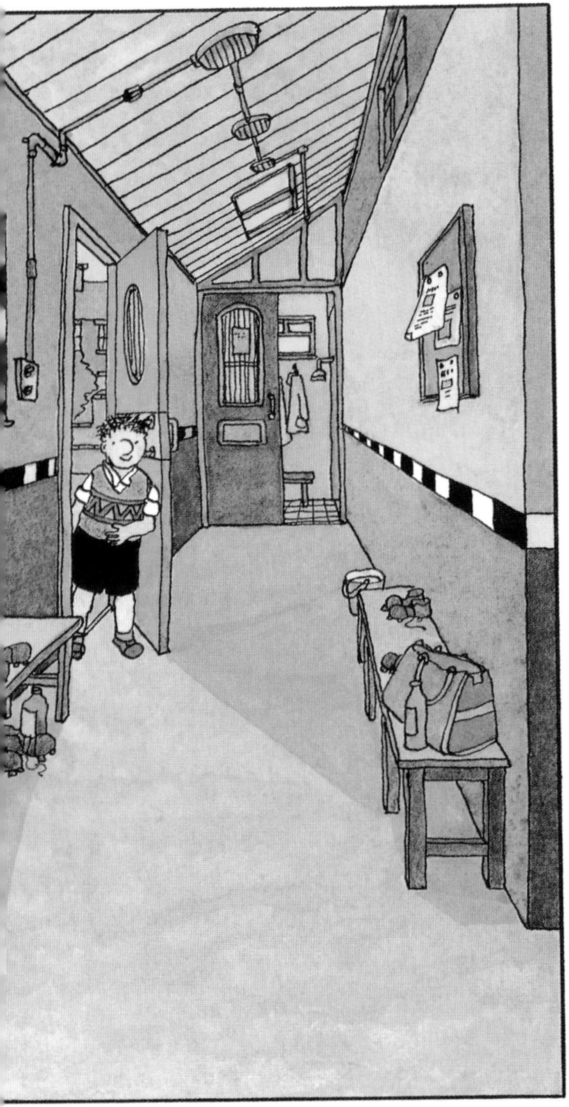

The changing-room was quite deserted.
Stan thought that it was really weird.

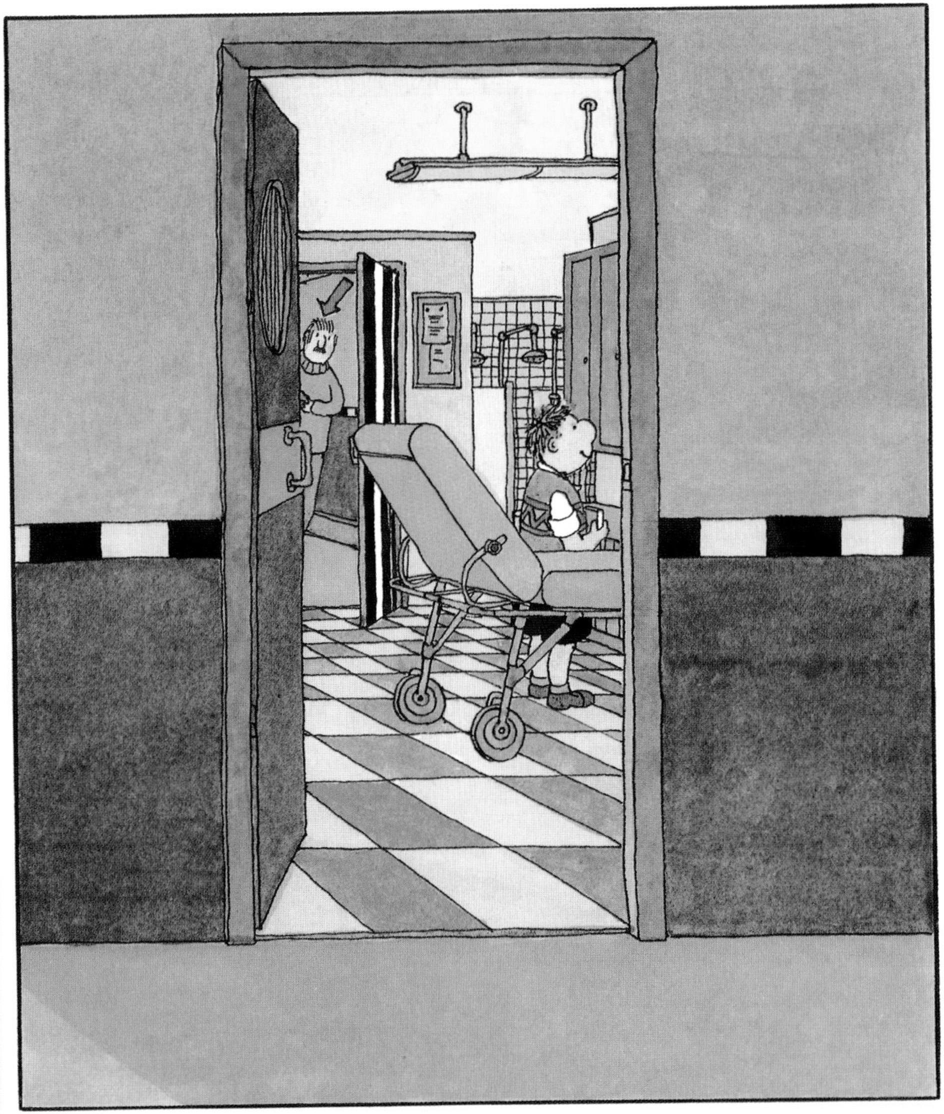

He went in to explore, but a shock was in store,
When the substitute goalie appeared.

And mistaking our Stan for a ball-boy,
He said ...

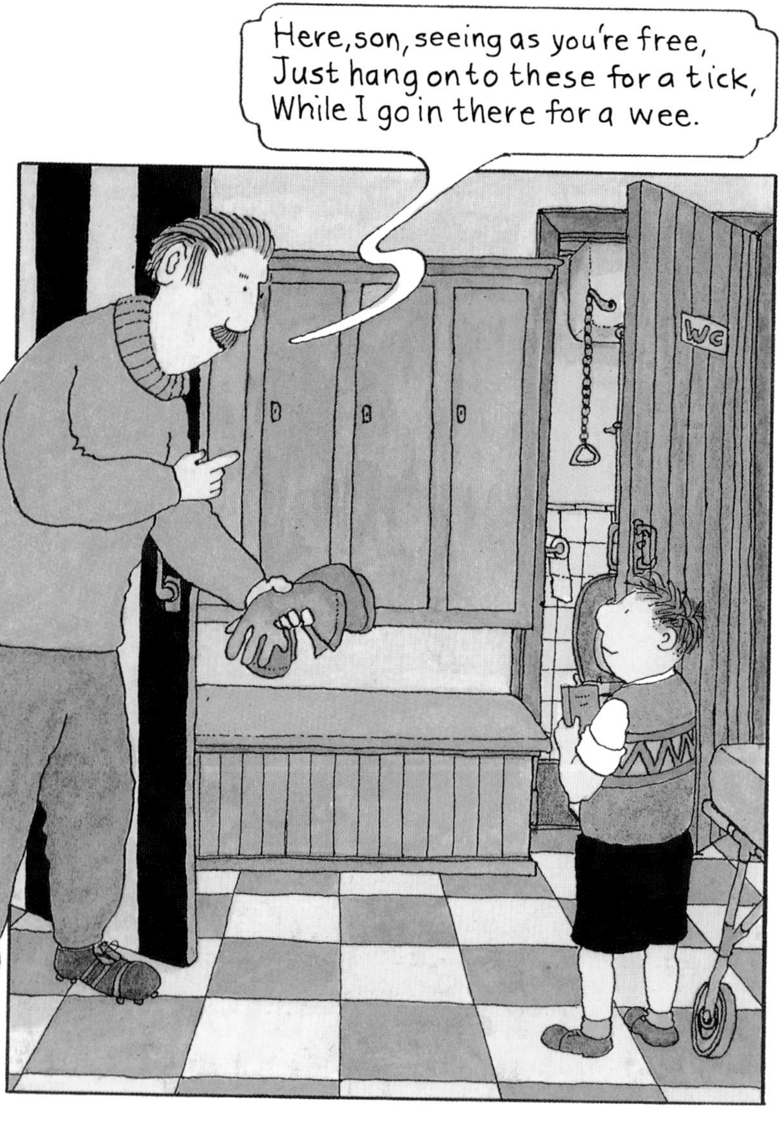
Here, son, seeing as you're free,
Just hang onto these for a tick,
While I go in there for a wee.
WC

When Stan saw
What the goalie had given him,
His little heart went pitter-pat.

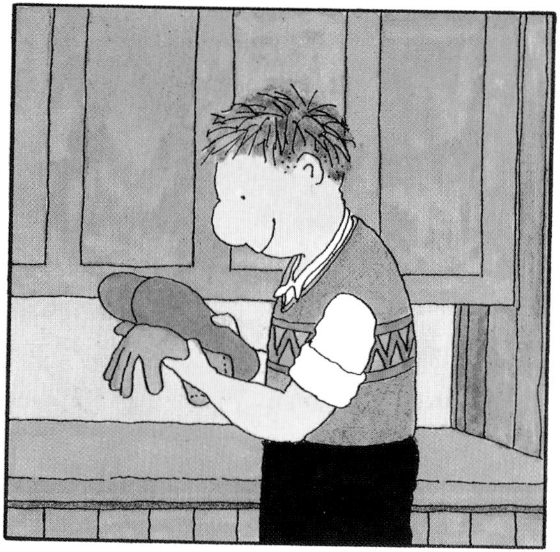

For there he was,
holding real goalkeeper's gloves,
And a genuine goalkeeper's hat.

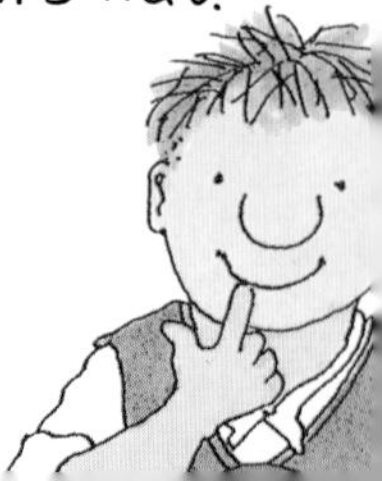

Meanwhile: outside, the tension was mounting.
There were only five minutes to go.
Could the Huddersgate team hold onto its lead?
(The Albion fans didn't know.)

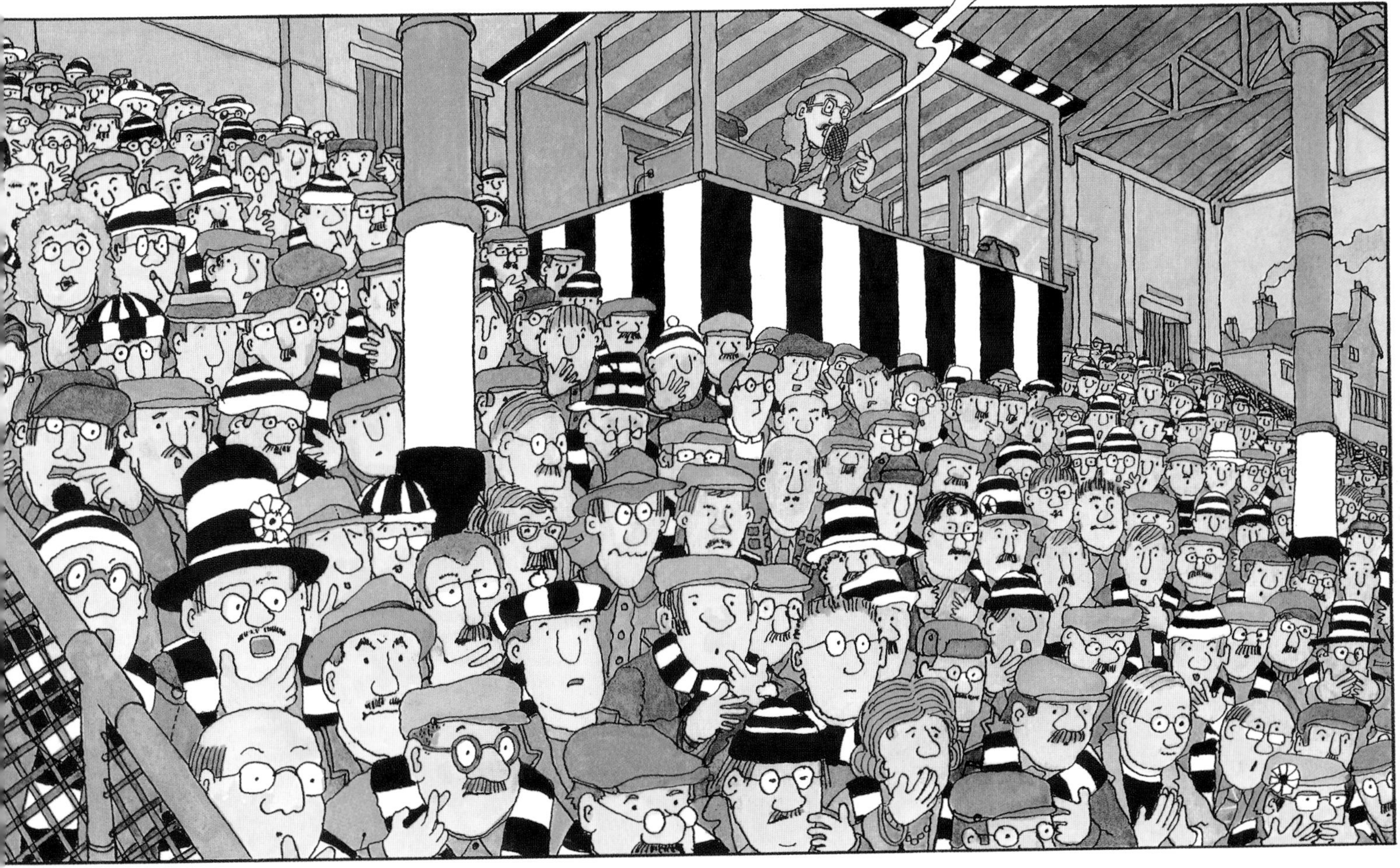
Yes-'can they hold out?'-that's the question. They certainly are on the rack. As the ball is pumped into the Albion half, And Spurs mount another attack!

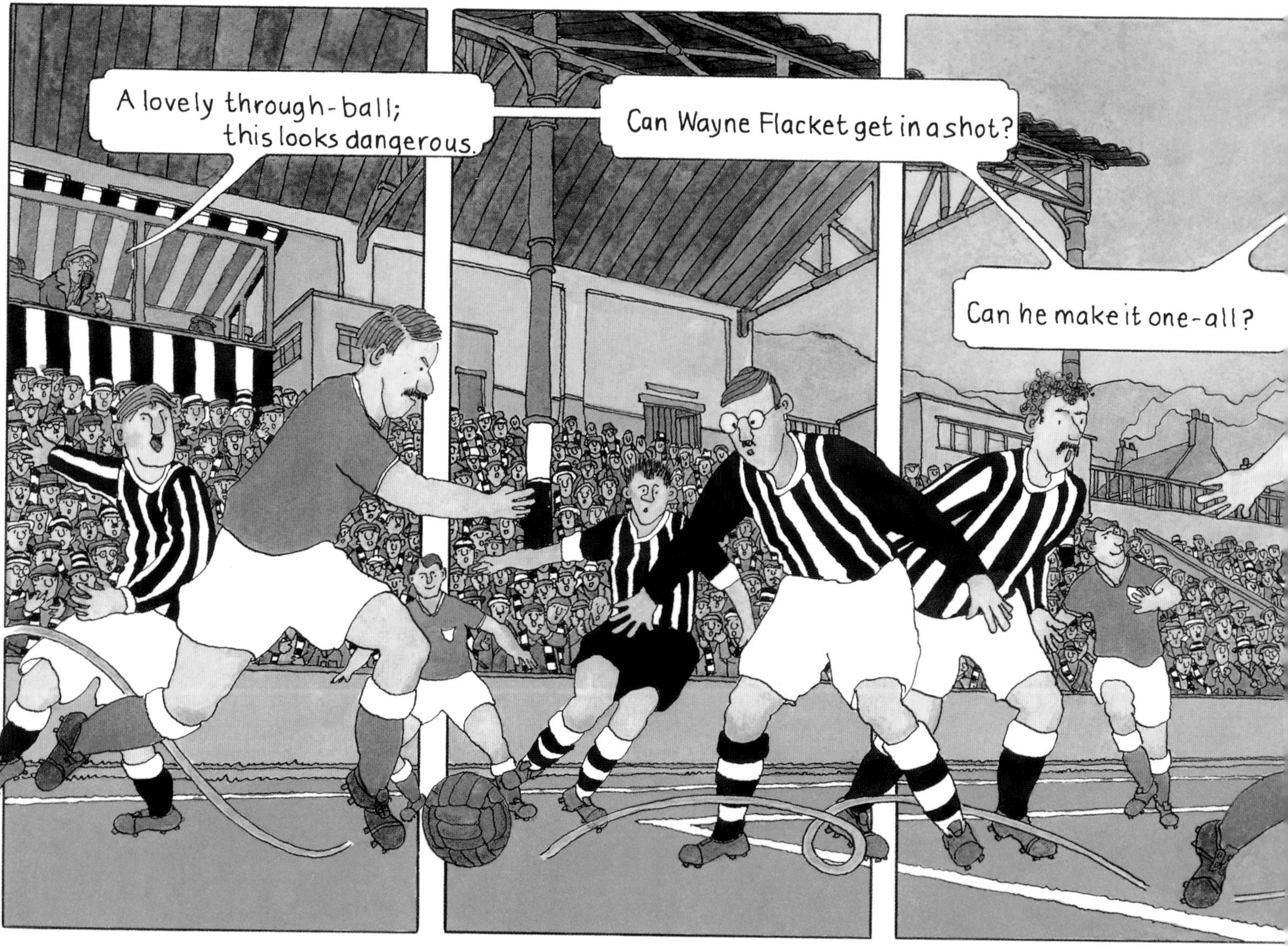
A lovely through-ball;
this looks dangerous.
Can Wayne Flacket get in a shot?
Can he make it one-all?

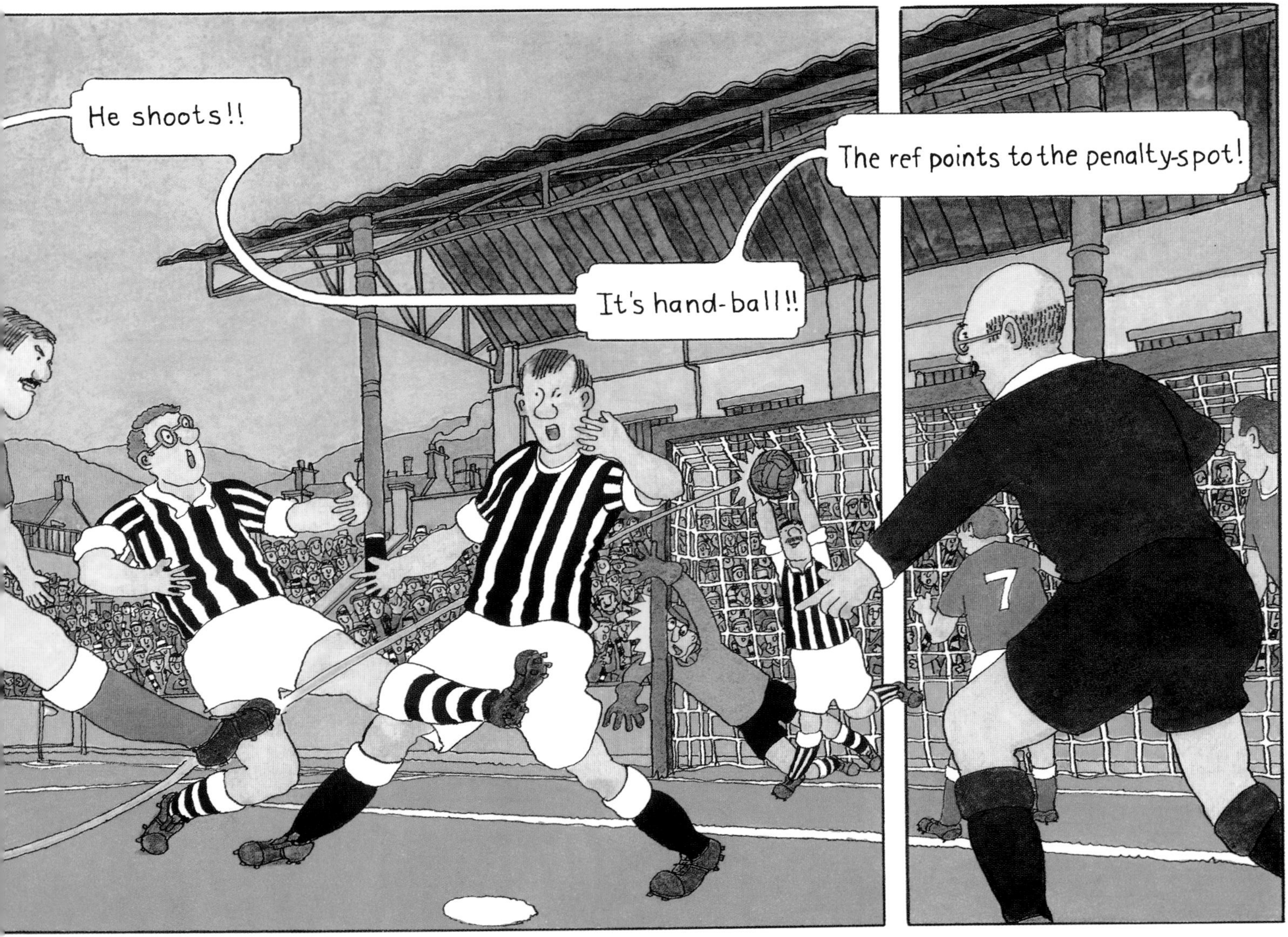
He shoots!!
It's hand-ball!!
The ref points to the penalty-spot!
7

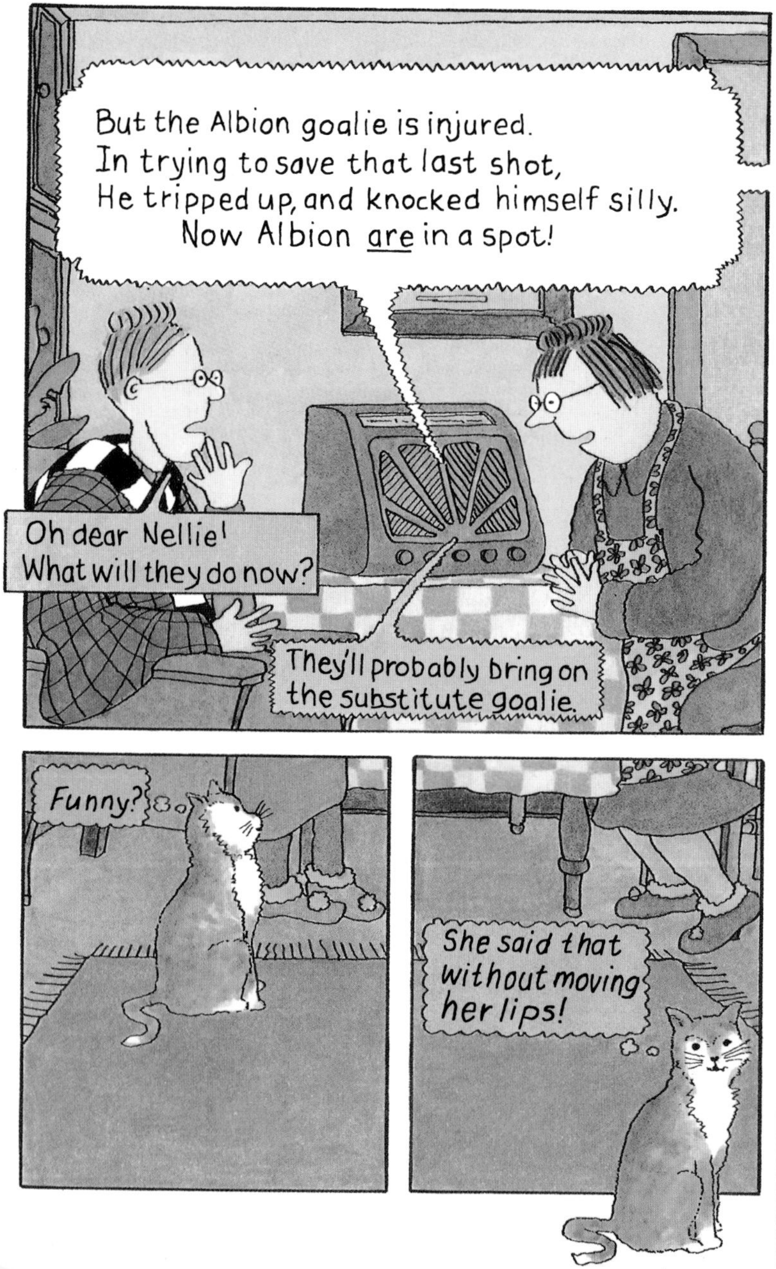
But the Albion goalie is injured. In trying to save that last shot, He tripped up, and knocked himself silly. Now Albion are in a spot!
Oh dear Nellie! What will they do now?
They'll probably bring on the substitute goalie.
Funny?
She said that without moving her lips!

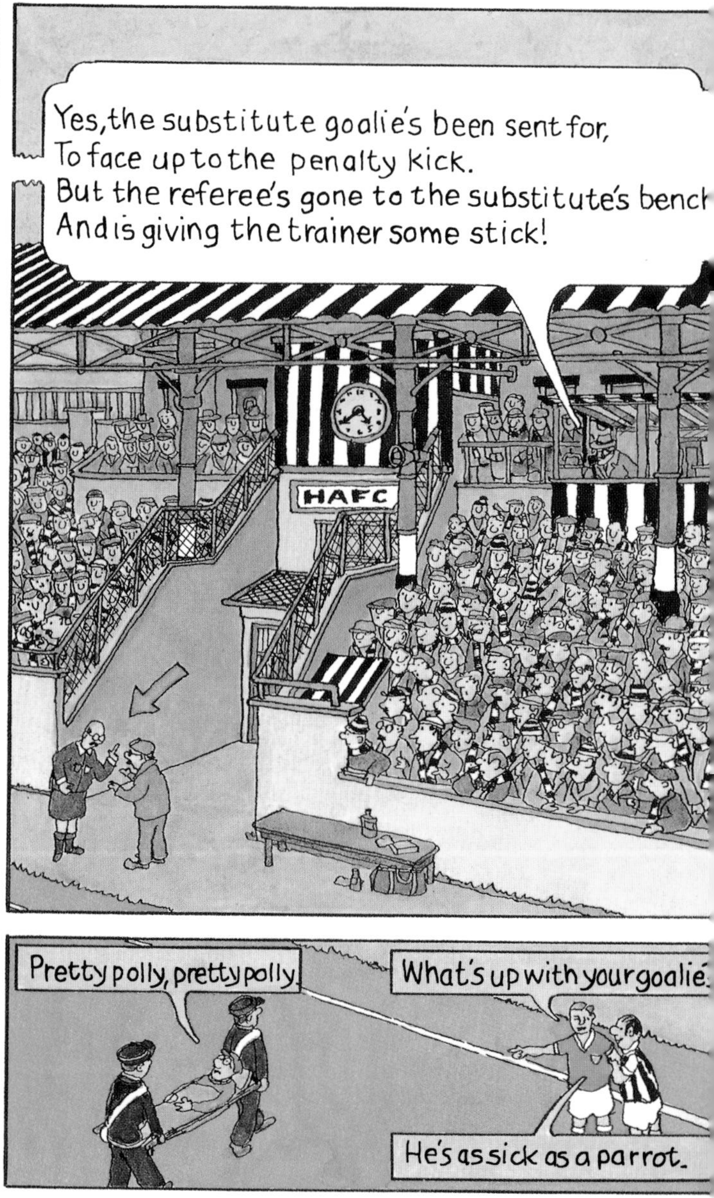
Yes, the substitute goalie's been sent for, To face up to the penalty kick. But the referee's gone to the substitute's benc And is giving the trainer some stick!
HAFC
Pretty polly, pretty polly.
What's up with your goalie
He's as sick as a parrot.

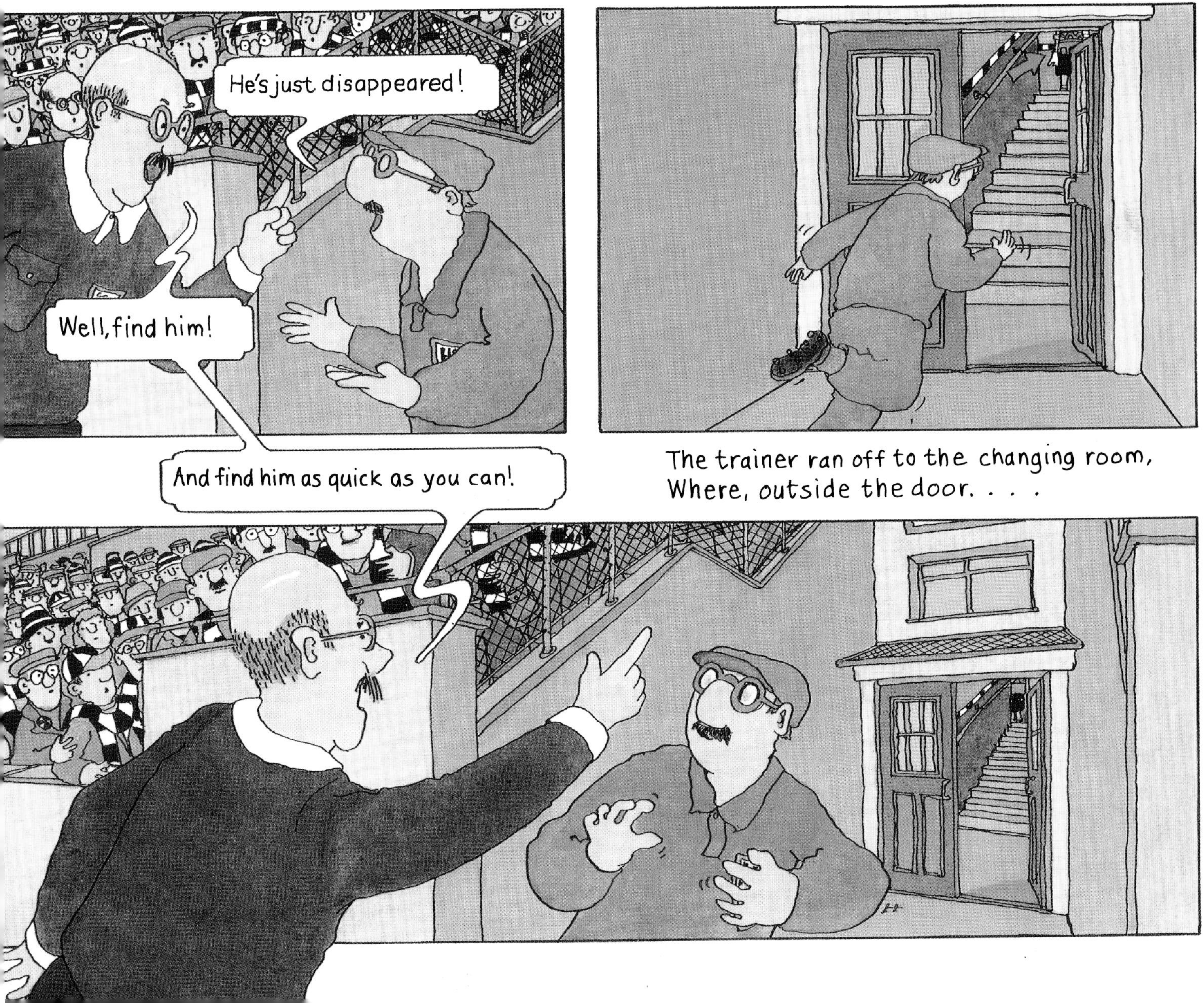
He's just disappeared!
Well, find him!
And find him as quick as you can!
The trainer ran off to the changing room,
Where, outside the door. . . .

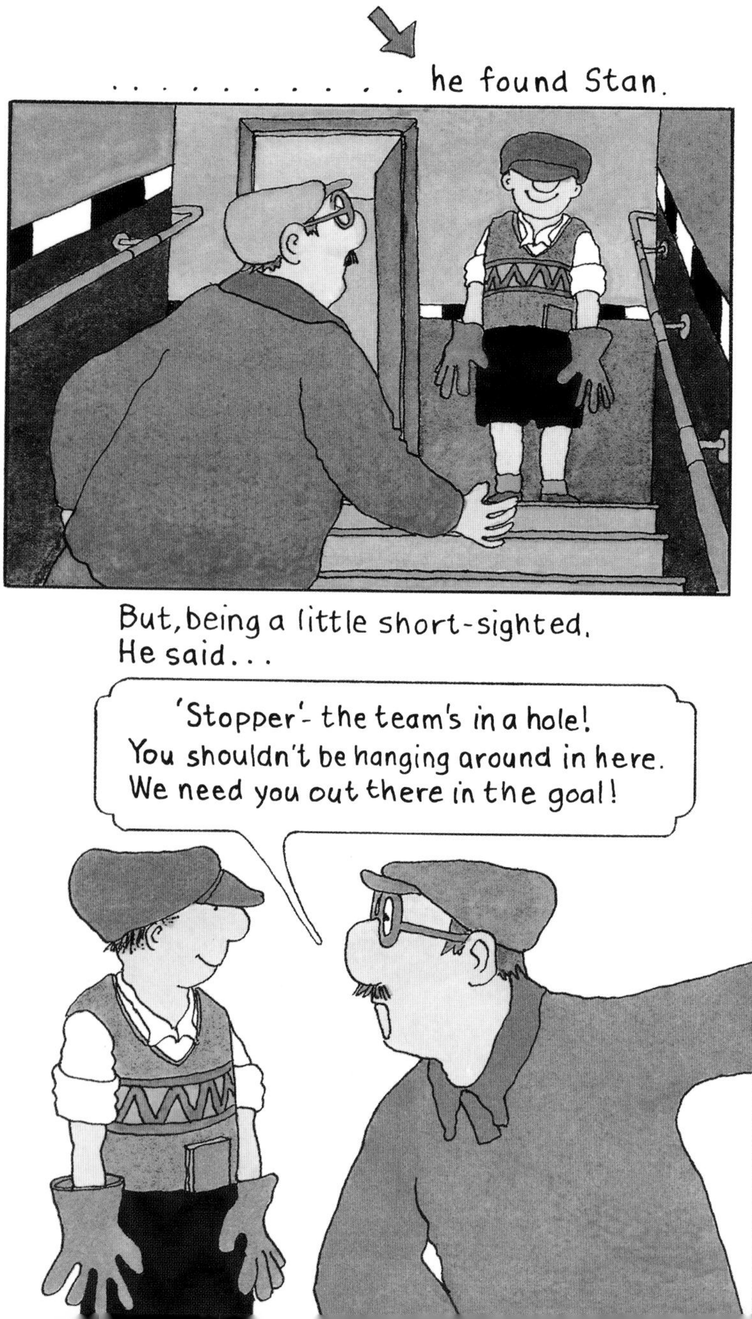
. . . . he found Stan.
But, being a little short-sighted,
He said . . .
'Stopper'- the team's in a hole!
You shouldn't be hanging around in here.
We need you out there in the goal!

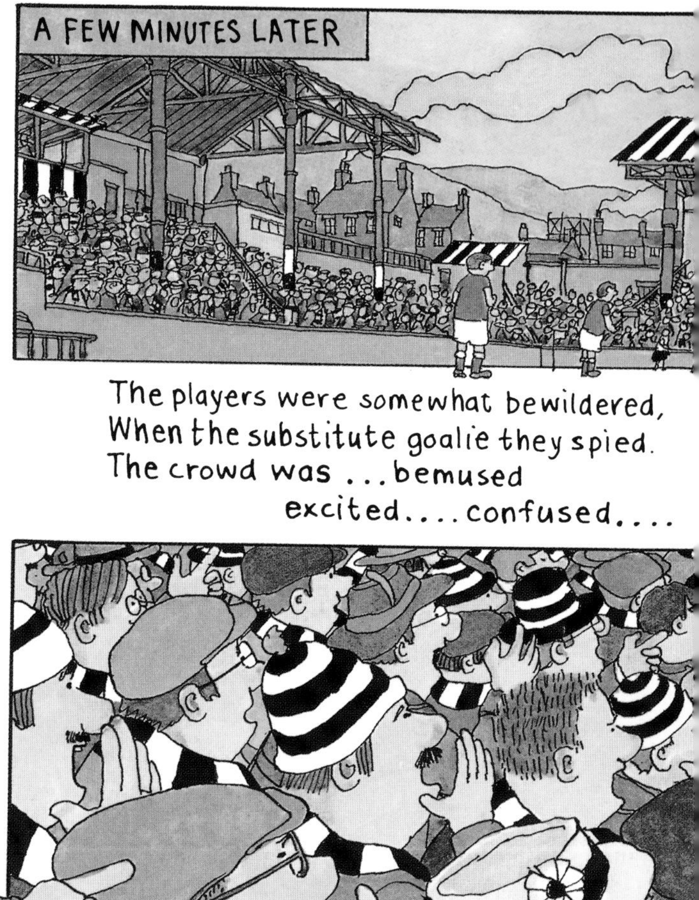
A FEW MINUTES LATER
The players were somewhat bewildered,
When the substitute goalie they spied.
The crowd was . . . bemused
excited. . . . confused. . . .

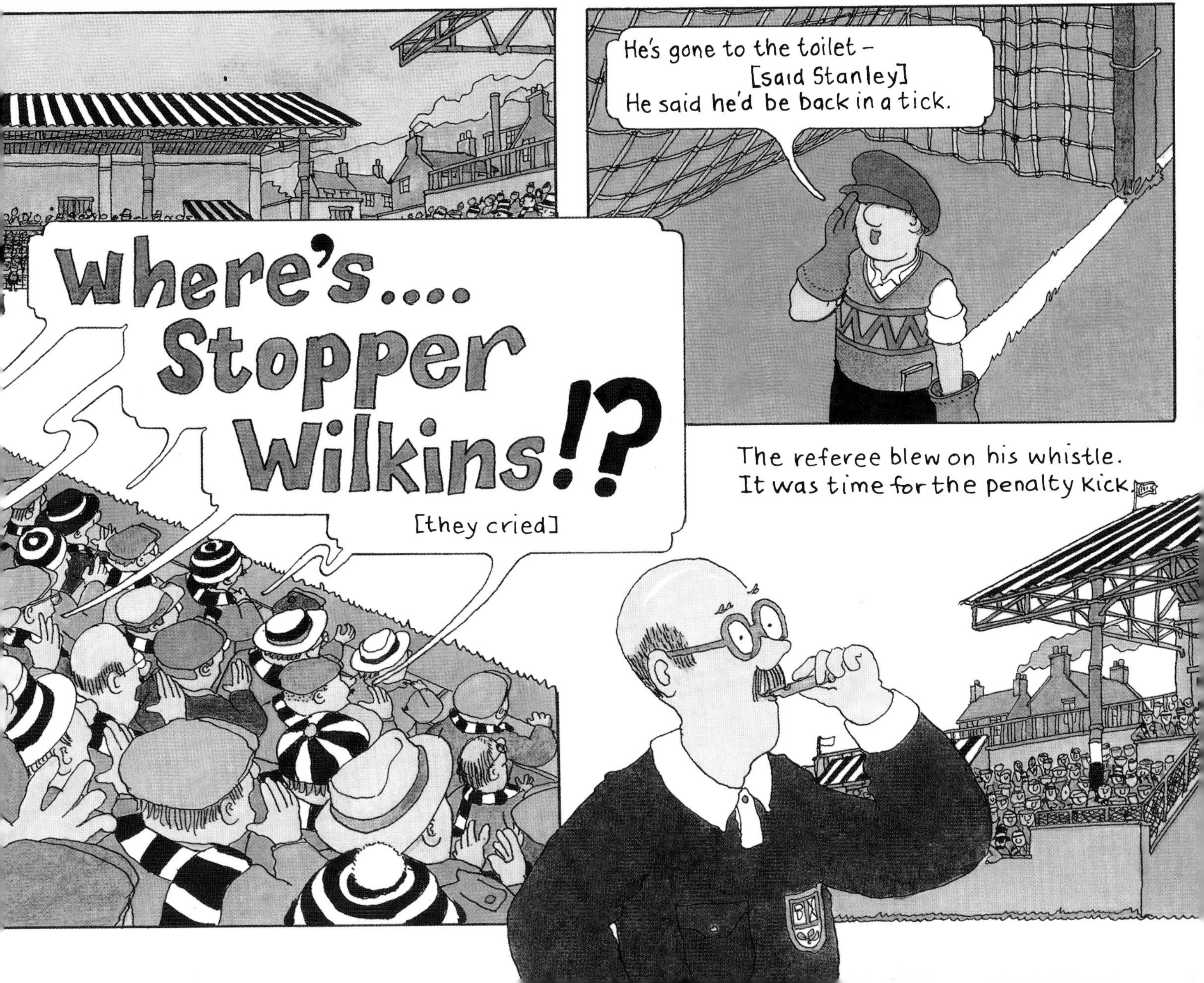
Where's.... Stopper Wilkins!?
[they cried]
He's gone to the toilet – [said Stanley] He said he'd be back in a tick.
The referee blew on his whistle. It was time for the penalty kick.

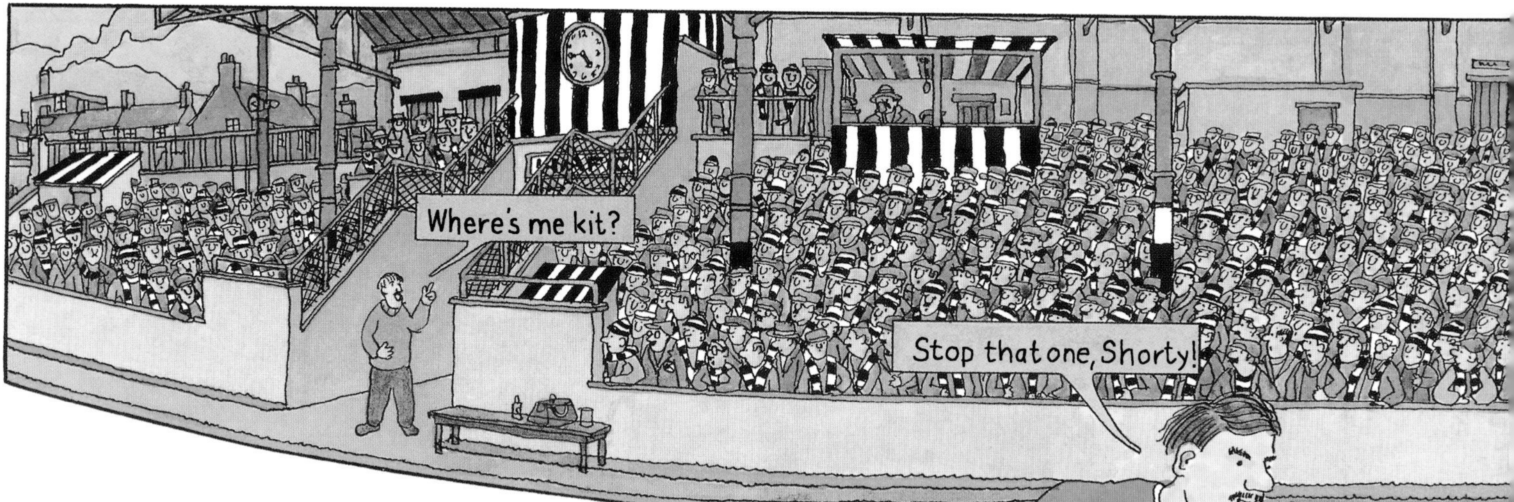
Where's me kit?
Stop that one, Shorty!

Stopper Wilkins appeared on the touchline.
And, seeing our Stan, gave a shout.
As Wayne Flacket ran up like an express train

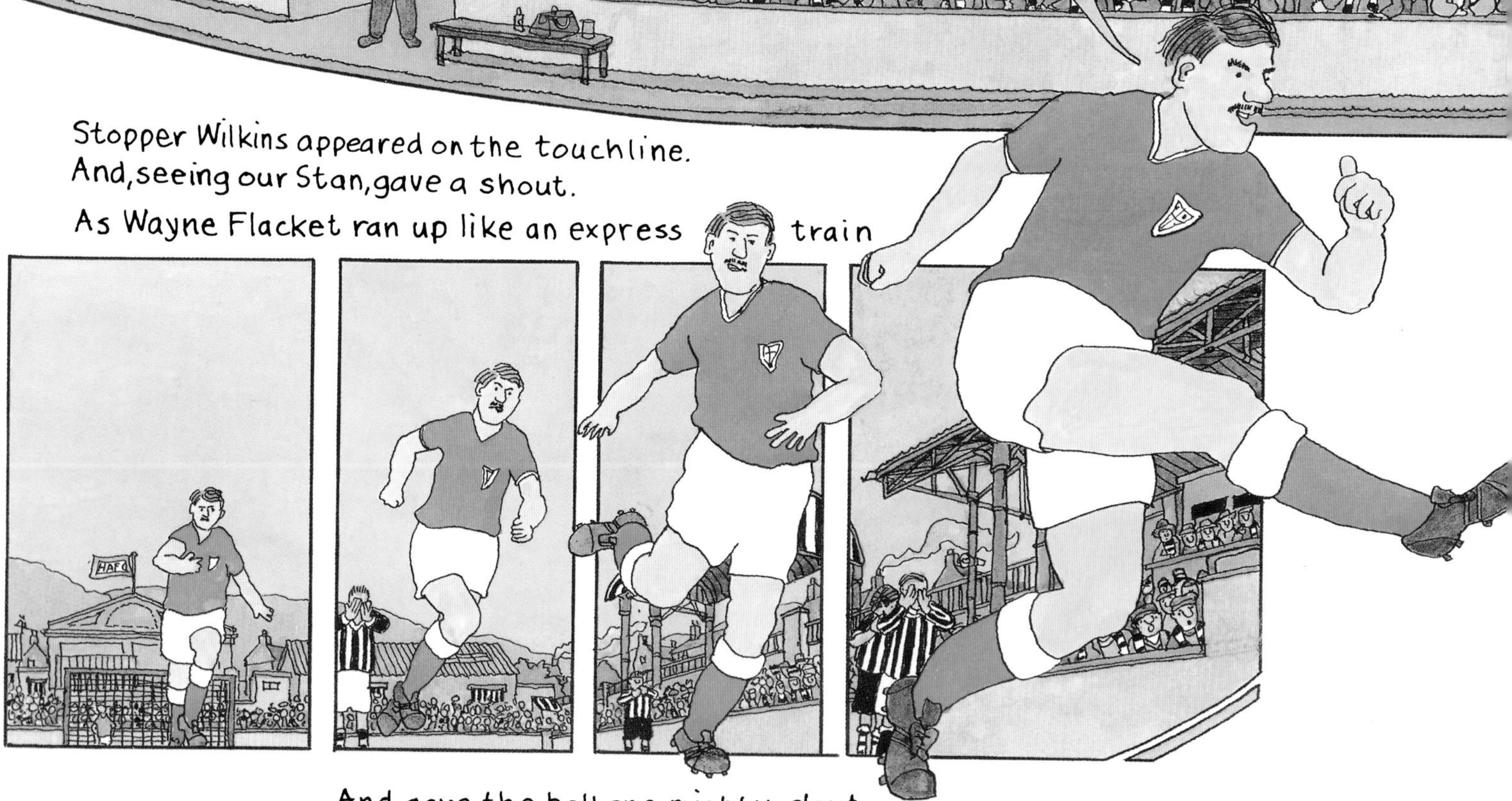
HAFC

And gave the ball one mighty clout.

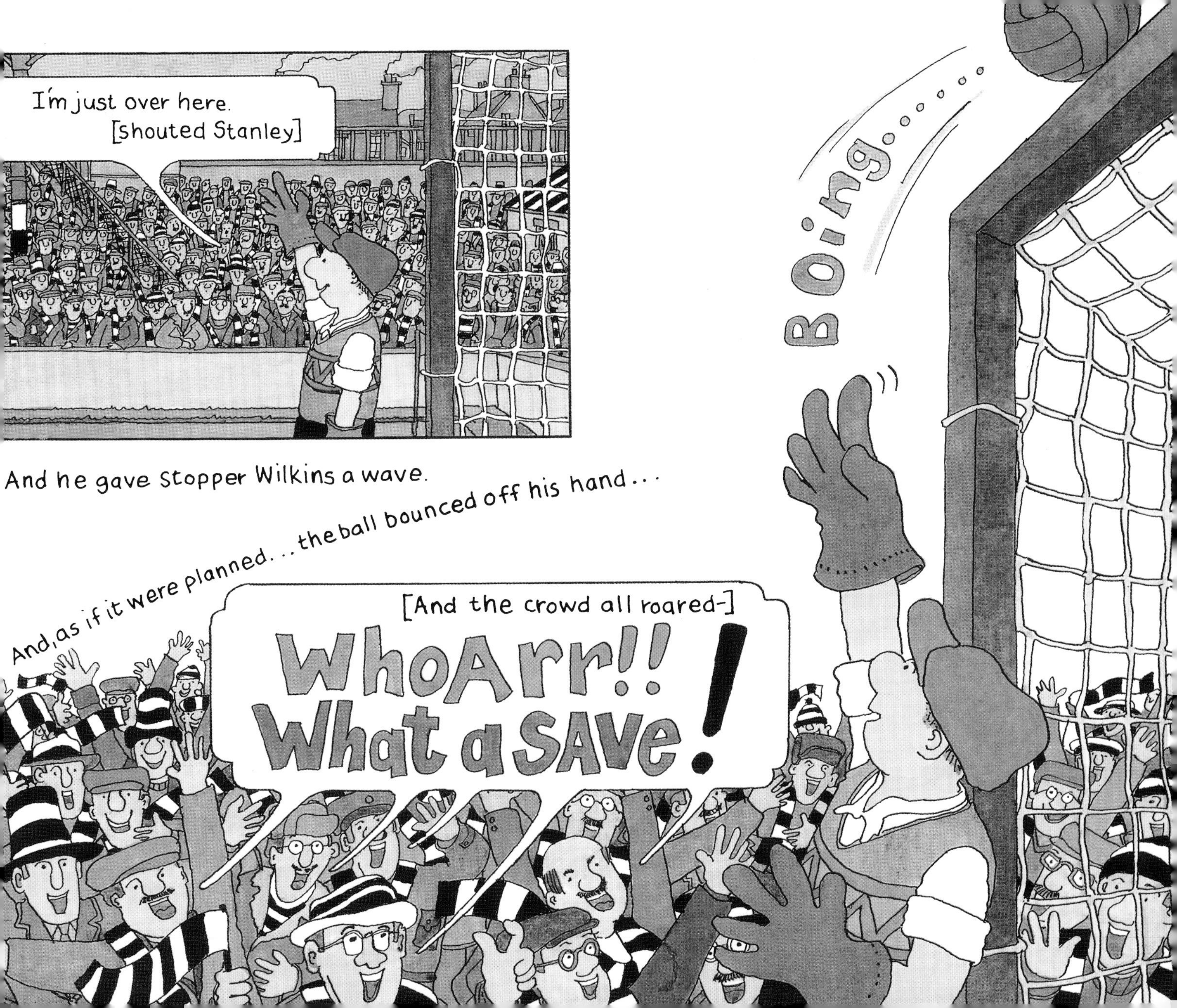
I'm just over here.
[shouted Stanley]
And he gave Stopper Wilkins a wave.
And, as if it were planned. . . the ball bounced off his hand . . .
BOing. . . . . . .
[And the crowd all roared-]
WhoArr!! What a SAVE!

The ref blew the final whistle.
The Albion players gave a shout...

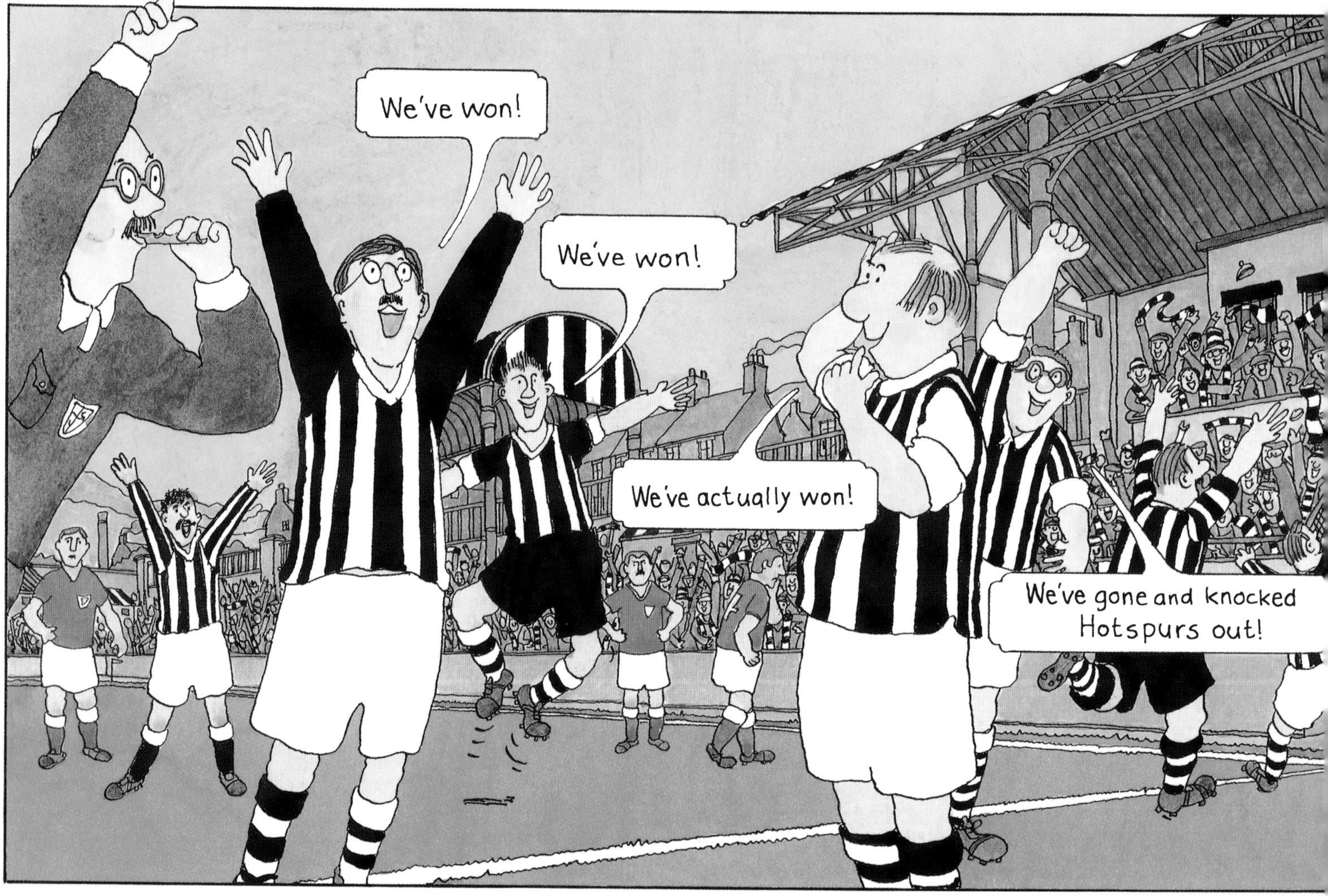
We've won!
We've won!
We've actually won!
We've gone and knocked Hotspurs out!

They ran round the pitch, all excited
And waving their hands at the sky.

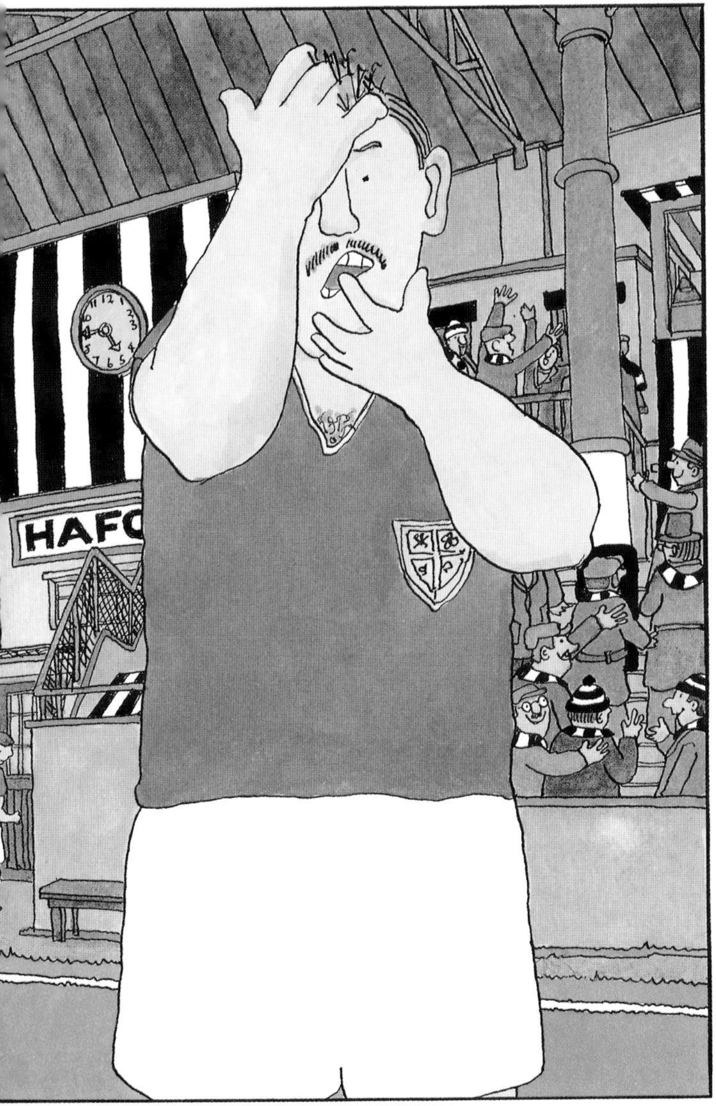
HAFC

While Wayne Flacket, the penalty taker
Was doing his best not to cry.

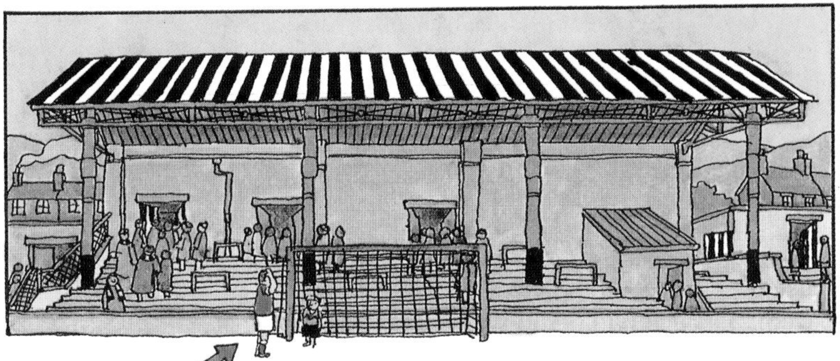

He couldn't believe what had happened.
Just stood there, as if in a trance.

Stan noticed the world-renowned player
And thought to himself...

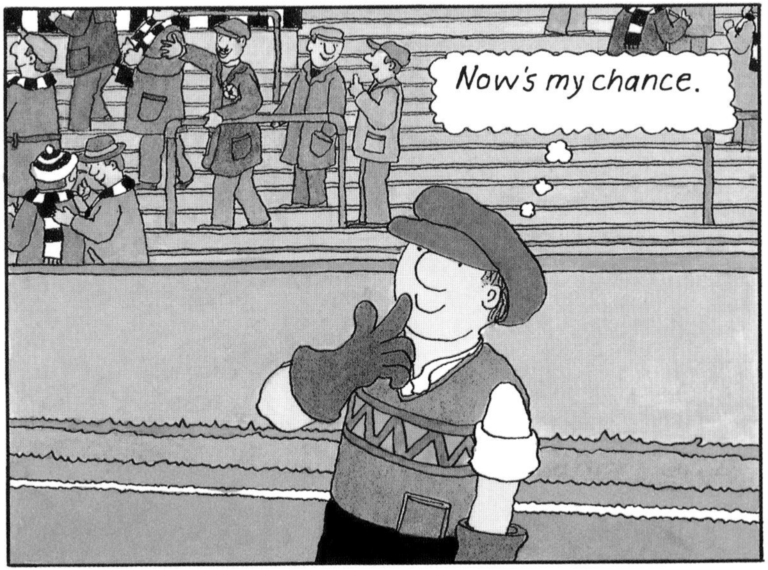
Now's my chance.

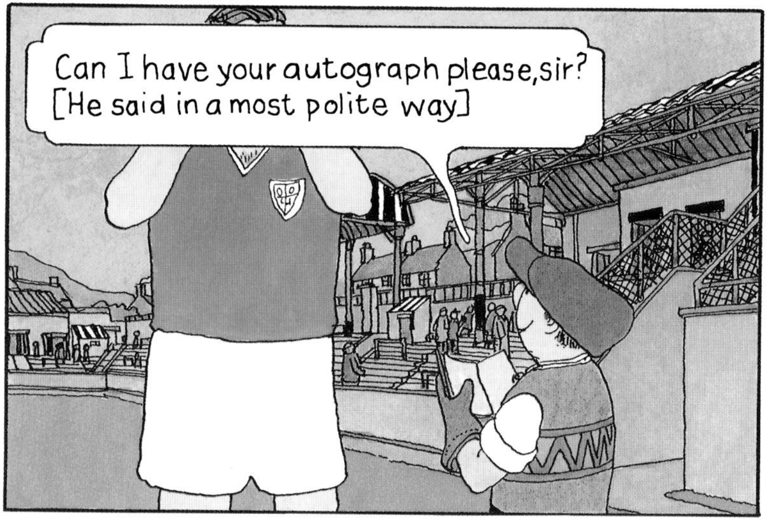
Can I have your autograph please,sir?
[He said in a most polite way]

Wayne replied-

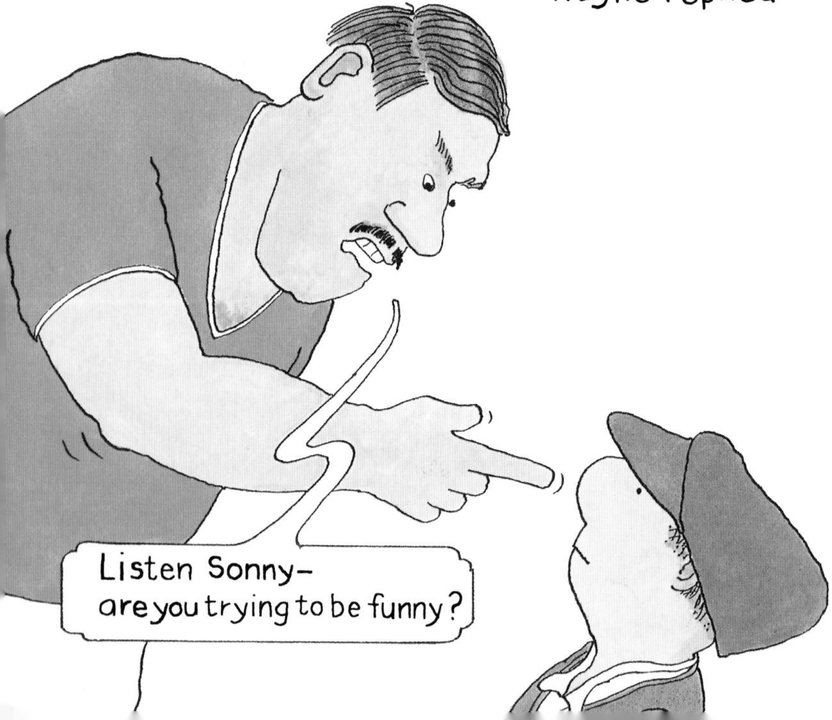
Listen Sonny-
are you trying to be funny?

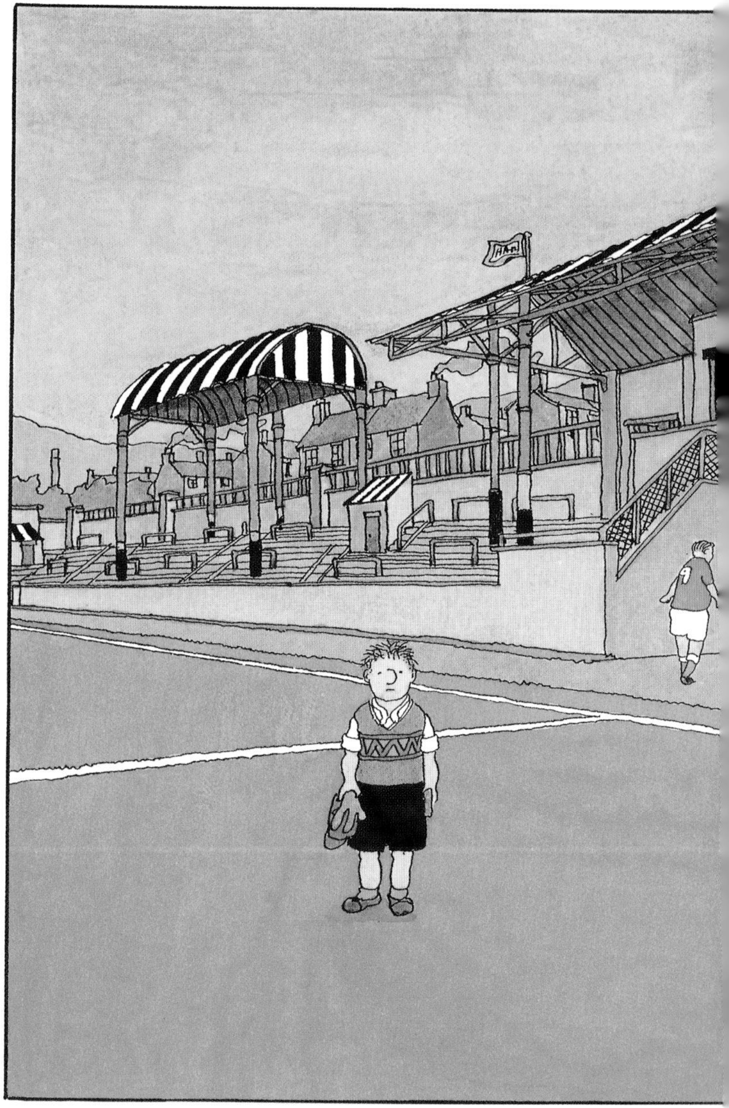

And our Stan didn't know what to say.

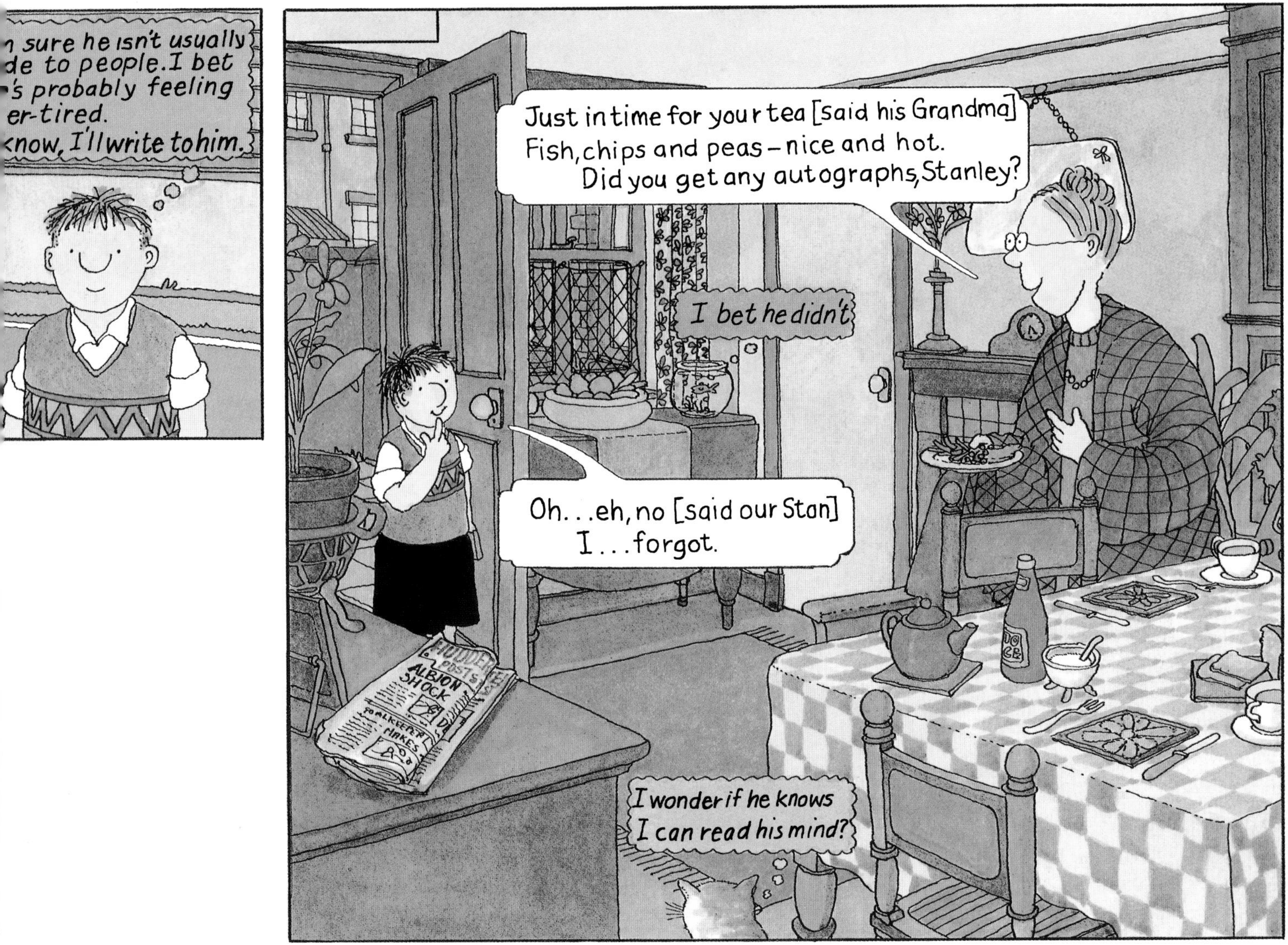
sure he isn't usually
de to people. I bet
's probably feeling
er-tired.
know, I'll write to him.
Just in time for your tea [said his Grandma] Fish, chips and peas – nice and hot. Did you get any autographs, Stanley?
I bet he didn't
Oh...eh, no [said our Stan] I...forgot.
ALBION SHOCK
I wonder if he knows I can read his mind?

NOT QUITE THE END

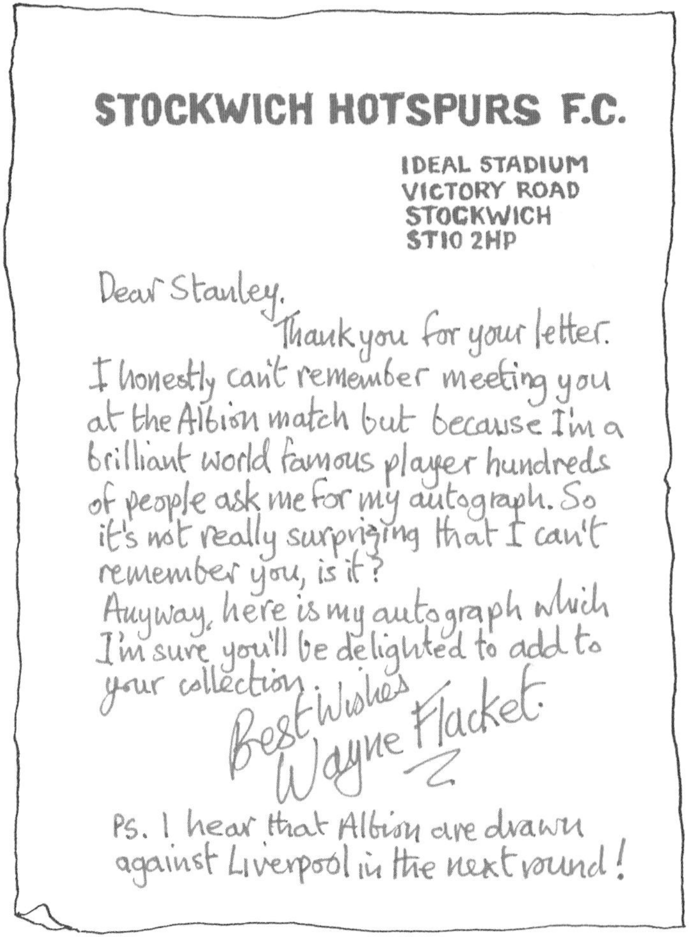

STOCKWICH HOTSPURS F.C.

**IDEAL STADIUM
VICTORY ROAD
STOCKWICH
ST10 2HP**

Dear Stanley,

Thank you for your letter.
I honestly can't remember meeting you
at the Albion match but because I'm a
brilliant world famous player hundreds
of people ask me for my autograph. So
it's not really surprising that I can't
remember you, is it?

Anyway, here is my autograph which
I'm sure you'll be delighted to add to
your collection.

Best Wishes
Wayne Flacket.

PS. I hear that Albion are drawn
against Liverpool in the next round!

THE END

First published by Hamish Hamilton Children's Books 1986
Text and pictures copyright © Bob Wilson 1986, 2003
This edition published 2003 by Barn Owl Books, 157 Fortis Green Road, London N10 3LX
Barn Owl Books are distributed by Frances Lincoln, 4 Torriano Mews, Torriano Avenue, London NW5 2RZ
ISBN 1-903015-26-X

Designed by Douglas Martin
Printed and bound in China